Kathie Deviny (handwritten signature)

Death in the Memorial Garden

KATHIE DEVINY

Seattle, WA

Camel Press
PO Box 70515
Seattle, WA 98127

For more information go to: www.camelpress.com
Deviny.camelpress.com

Cover design by Sabrina Sun

Death in the Memorial Garden
Copyright © 2013 Kathie Deviny

ISBN: 978-1-60381-899-5 (Trade Paper)
ISBN: 978-1-60381-900-8 (eBook)

Library of Congress Control Number: 2012941565

Printed in the United States of America

Death in the Memorial Garden

This book is dedicated to ...
Family, Friends and Fellow Writers
The People of Trinity Parish
and
Paul

How they so softly rest

Chapter 1

The pigeons were gathering on the lawn of the Memorial Garden, just as they always seemed to do before an internment. Father Robert Vickers, the rector of Grace Episcopal Church, watched the birds peck, preen and flutter.

The door of the church opened for a minute and then closed with a loud thud. A minute later it opened a second time, and once again thudded shut. Robert checked his watch and sighed. The mourners were obviously having a good time visiting inside the church, where the funeral service had been held. They probably were hoping he'd delay the internment until it stopped raining. He didn't mind, really. It was his first quiet moment all day.

God bless old Reverend Lewis, Robert thought. In the 1970s, his distant predecessor, using skills gained in his former career as an attorney, had shepherded a law through the state legislature breaking the monopoly of the cemeteries on burials. Robert liked to think of it as the "Hallowed Ground" law. Since then, the patch of lawn beside the church had become a burial ground for the ashes of its deceased.

Despite his satisfaction with the presence of the Memorial Garden at his parish, Robert was not a happy man. His bad mood wasn't because of the be-pigeoned lawn, or the spring downpour that made the birds' feathers sodden and the ground soggy. If pigeons or rain had the power to make

1

people unhappy, everyone in Seattle would be suicidal. Nor was it because of the internment service he was preparing to conduct. Neola Peterson had lived the full measure of her days, enjoying every minute and, it was rumored, had willed a tidy sum to the church. Her ashes would soon be joining those of her beloved husband Fred, who had died last year.

If he could devote more time to marrying and burying, visiting the sick, clothing the naked and feeding the hungry, he'd be a happy man. And if the Holy Spirit would blow his way a woman willing to marry a 5'10," middle-aged, balding clergyman with thick glasses, he'd be ecstatic. No, what was making him unhappy today was more concrete. Bricks and mortar, to be exact—the crumbling bricks and mortar of Grace Church's bell tower.

He was in the middle of a fight with the vestry over fixing the unstable structure looming over the Memorial Garden. They didn't want to spend money the congregation didn't have, and the Bishop felt the same way. Robert's superior would gladly disband the small congregation and sell the property. Never mind that it was the oldest church in the area, that the ashes of the famous dead of the city were interred in the altar, that its pipe organ and German stained glass were renowned far and wide. What good was all that, they all but said, when the average Sunday attendance in the 400-person sanctuary was sixty, and the average age seventy, with ten of the congregation pushing 100?

One of the new vestry members, a businessman in his thirties who worked in a high-rise downtown, had come up with a scheme he claimed would solve all their problems. It involved selling what he called an "underutilized" part of their property to a real estate developer, who would build a tall, skinny condo. Apparently, Grace Church owned thousands of square feet of underutilized empty air above its roof that could be transmigrated one half block north to add ten stories of concrete to the city height limit. Robert hoped there'd be room for him in the condo, because the underutilized corner included the rectory. It also included the food bank, which he seriously doubted the developer would want to keep as an anchor tenant.

This vestry member, Rick, claimed that the church and the Memorial Garden would remain the same, and that proceeds from the sale could be used to fix the bell tower and create a healthy endowment. Robert smelled a rat, but he hadn't been able to flush it out—yet—and wished his seminary training had included a few business courses.

As he headed to summon the mourners, a brown lump in the corner of the garden caught Robert's attention. Protected by an overhang, the patch of soft lawn attracted urban campers.

Detouring, he called out, "Excuse me, sir," to the person inside the sleeping bag, "but you're lying in a graveyard and we're burying someone in a few minutes. You'll have to find somewhere else to sleep."

"The Hell you say!" came a voice from inside the bag. A head emerged. The man was about forty, with bushy dull brown hair and a matching week-old beard.

"Wait a minute!" the man said. "Where are the gravestones? You can't have a cemetery without gravestones!" He paused. "Just kidding, padre."

Robert answered, "Oh, it's you, Lester. You know better than to sleep here."

"Yeah, but this was an emergency. The mission was full, and so were all the best spaces under the freeway bridge. Besides, it's dangerous down there." Sitting up in the sleeping bag, he yawned hugely and cleared his throat. Seeing that he was preparing to spit, Father Robert scowled, so Lester swallowed instead and said, "This ground is too cold anyway. I'm heading to the steam grate on Second Avenue. Have to get my dibs in first. The other day two guys beat me to it. And they weren't even sleeping. They were looking at dirty

3

pictures on one of them little computers." Seeing Robert's skeptical frown, he added, "I'd swear it on a Bible if I had one."

Wondering where the pair recharged the computer's battery, Robert let Lester use the church bathroom. But first he warned him to tell his friends that if he heard of any more drug use in there, or vandalism, the privilege would be cut off. As the priest hurried toward the church, the scent of daffodils wafted under his nose, smoothing his furrowed brow. He smiled. It was a good day for a burial.

⌘

Rick Chase stood at the window of his twenty-fifth floor office. Mount Rainier wasn't out today, but he had a nice view of the bustling waterfront.

Up the hill just south and east, he could see Grace Church's shingled bell tower topped by a modest brass cross. The rest of the structure was hidden by a big public housing project and the public hospital. Not exactly the toniest part of town.

He and Stacy had been married there by Father Robert. Even though churches were no longer fashionable places for weddings, Stacy had insisted on Grace, because it was where her grandparents had exchanged vows, back before the mansions had been torn down and the town's movers and shakers had relocated to Capitol Hill and north to the Highlands.

Stacy was the churchgoer, not Rick, but he loved old buildings and wanted to save this one. That's why he'd joined the vestry and solicited the advice of real estate developer friends on a proposal to develop the property. He figured the area was due for a turnaround. He couldn't profit from the project directly, but its successful completion would save the structure and raise his profile in the business community.

At last week's downtown Rotary meeting he'd managed to sidle up to Bishop Anthony Adams. The man ("Call me Bishop Anthony, son!") was excited at the prospect of development. A tall condo plus a bigger cross on top of the church would increase the visibility of the Diocese, the Bishop said, and oh, Grace Church, of course.

Rick wondered if he should be attending the funeral scheduled for this afternoon. He didn't know the deceased, but had heard she had a pretty substantial estate. He could see who was there and introduce himself to her family. It would be good if some of the restoration funds came directly from the Parish. The development group would need their buy-in or things could get sticky.

He checked his phone and rubbed the top of his brown crew cut. If he skipped the funeral and just showed up at the internment, he'd have enough time to grab a sandwich as he walked up the hill.

Ê

Lucy Lawrence looked about her at the twenty other mourners standing in the Memorial Garden. The sight of the elderly women—dressed in somber wool coats and sober black chunky-heeled oxfords, umbrellas unfurled against the rain—did nothing to lift her spirits. They were here to bury Neola Peterson, their friend and contemporary. Neola would not have approved of the mourners' attire; she would have worn a mink wrap and spike heels to her funeral, even in the pouring rain.

I fit right in with the old ladies, Lucy thought, glancing down at her belted navy raincoat and zip up boots. She felt her limp hair separate around her ears, remembering Neola's soft ash curls tinged with pink, miles more stylish than her own gray pageboy. *Too bad she's gone*, Lucy mused. *I'll miss her. But she was eighty-eight after all, and I'm not far behind.*

One can't go on forever, Lucy told herself sternly, *and I for one wouldn't care to.*

Just the previous week Neola had attended the cake and coffee party for Lucy's seventy-eighth birthday. It was her last public appearance. Immediately after returning to her suite, the unfortunate woman had suffered a stroke and spent her final days in the first floor nursing center, dressed in a horrible backless cotton thing. Lucy would be satisfied to die in her own bed.

The square of lawn surrounded by loose earth and plantings that constituted the Memorial Garden was creased with brown, soggy footprints. The branches of the rhododendrons on its perimeter drooped under their load of showy blossoms. The rhodies here always bloomed a month ahead of schedule.

Looming to the immediate south, the century-old shingle and stone church blocked what little light there was on this blustery day. The bell tower seemed to shiver as the wind whistled through its shuttered window openings. To Lucy's right and immediately to the north, the steam-heated parish hall beckoned. She spied the tea urn and trays of cookies through the French doors.

Watching the pigeons flapping around reminded Lucy of her parents' Iowa chicken coop, and the memory filled her nostrils briefly with its dusty, acrid odor. She sniffed, and the smell was gone, neutralized by the moist, cool Northwest air.

As the mourners hunched into their coats, Father Robert, water dripping off his balding head, started to read the burial service at double speed, garbling the stately phrases.

"'N the midst oflife we're in death whomayweseek for succor butoftheeoLord?"

Why doesn't he shave that mustache? Lucy grumbled silently to herself. *It doesn't disguise the fact that he's over fifty and it turns his speech to mush!* There was nothing he could do about the lack of forehead hair, of course. *Why, he looks a bit like Brother Cadfael*, she realized, *except that his tonsure stops at his ears.* Her irritation dissipated as she recalled with pleasure the Ellis Peters mysteries about the twelfth century English monk "with a past," who solved murders related to the turbulent politics of the time.

She wondered why religious mysteries almost always featured monks or priests rather than the descendants of Martin Luther or John Calvin. Possibly they considered solving crimes a distraction from Bible Study.

Speaking of distraction, she willed herself to focus on the matter at hand. Neola's ashes were being interred next to her late husband's ... at least where they were supposed to be. One might wonder after that unfortunate incident last year. Lucy smiled, remembering the congregation's outrage upon discovering that an over-enthusiastic groundskeeper had removed the sod and six inches of topsoil to level the area. Although Father had reassured them repeatedly that the remains were buried at least a foot deep, suspicion lingered that the garden's previous occupants were now reposing at the city composting facility.

Lucy spotted her own 144 square inches, a few feet to the left of Neola's. She'd purchased it after retiring from the Midwest to Seattle to be near her widowed brother Thomas and her niece Lisa. Her retirement residence was near Grace Church, which had been her brother's parish for years. Thomas' plot was toward the middle of the garden. He hadn't given it up, even though he and Lisa were no longer members.

Since Lucy's estrangement from them the previous spring, they'd stopped attending. The thought of resting near Thomas for all eternity wasn't appealing, but of course it wouldn't matter then. People assumed that they'd moved or lost interest in religion, and she didn't disabuse them; she didn't want to increase her pain by sharing the truth.

The truth was that she had been overeager to share in the life of an active teenager who was also a musical prodigy. Thomas was a famous organist and Lisa had followed in his footsteps, amazing audiences with her mastery of the unwieldy instrument.

Thomas kept tight reigns on his daughter's practice and concert schedule. Only her high school studies were higher priority. Things had come to a head when Lucy planned an out of town trip for the two of them during Lisa's spring vacation. Because Lisa would have missed two rehearsals, Thomas refused to let her go. His inflexibility led to an ugly confrontation and then the estrangement.

As the service continued, Lucy remembered how much Father Vickers, despite his mustache and relative youth, had helped her after she stumbled into his office to share her grief and loss. Through their talks, she'd come from a place of despair to a shaky faith that "all would be well," just not on her timetable. At her invitation, he'd taken to visiting with her once a month at Heritage House, after his service for the shut-ins, even accepting a glass of sherry accompanied by water crackers. It was good to have a rector who appreciated the niceties.

He'd also encouraged her to call him "Robert," not that she was special in that regard. Upon appointment as their rector five years earlier, he'd told the congregation to dispense with the Father-this and Father-that. However, like most of Grace's parishioners, she had been raised in a more formal era. They compromised by calling him "Father" or "Father Robert" among themselves. However, it was always "Father Vickers" to strangers.

If my kitties predecease me, she thought, *I'll ask Father if their ashes can be buried with mine.* Blind, dumb animal love was the best, she'd decided long ago. Surely the Almighty would agree, after all the trouble He'd had over the centuries with the rest of creation. And if Father wouldn't allow it, she just might give away her plot and join her kitties in the charming pet garden located on the terraced area below the church's south side.

Other than a youngish, slender man with a brown crew cut dressed in what looked like a Burberry raincoat, and the new young organist (who'd acquitted himself quite nicely during the funeral, pulling out all the stops, as it were), Neola's two teenaged grandchildren were the only mourners under thirty in attendance. The young man and woman seemed distinctly uncomfortable standing in a public place amidst people in long robes and underneath an oversized cross waving back and forth in the none-too-steady grip of old George the crucifer. Lucy noticed them glancing toward the street, fearing, she supposed, that a friend in a passing car might recognize them. The girl was just a few years older than her niece Lisa, she realized. A surge of longing welled up and she wiped away a tear. She missed Lisa terribly.

ର

After the last prayer before the actual burial of the ashes, Father Robert looked at the deceased's daughter and her husband, who seemed uncomfortable, apparently not having inherited Neola and Fred's dedication to the ways of the traditional church. He glanced at the service bulletin for their names, Mark and Audrey Miller. They seemed to be exactly the same height, about his 5'10". The husband was unremarkable, a middle-aged, middle-sized, brown-headed man. The wife was somewhat more handsome and stood up straight despite her height, as if she'd attended a poise class at some point.

Robert remembered Neola bemoaning their attendance at a Christian Center in the suburbs, where waving arms abounded but nary a waving cross could be seen. Neola blamed her daughter's new husband for, as she put it, "brainwashing" her.

He'd visited a number of these places incognito, when he relocated to Northwest Washington. He wanted to know how they attracted so many families so willing to part with the sums of money needed to maintain the large campus and multitudinous programs. The services reminded him of charity telethons, alternating professional quality musicians and sound systems with upbeat monologues by handsome pastors striding across the stage with mics stuck in their ears. *To each their own*, he finally decided.

Neola would also be mortified that the Millers' funeral attire consisted of blue jeans and windbreakers. The couple looked none too happy, either. Neola had promised a bequest to the church, and each seemed to be the type who would begrudge the loss of a few thousand dollars to charity.

Henry, the church caretaker, given the important title of "sexton" on occasions like this, was about to plunge a shovel into the soggy ground. The matching shirt and pants worn by the stocky, steel-gray-haired man presented quite a contrast to the white robes worn by the priest, deacon and crucifer. Ordinarily the hole itself was dug ahead of time and covered by a piece of turf, but in her funeral instructions Neola had opted for as much drama as possible.

Father Robert had to hand off the black plastic box containing Neola's ashes to his deacon, Mary, in order to read the next part of the internment service. As he recited the familiar words, "In sure and certain hope of the resurrection ...." he mused upon the role of the deacon, which he regarded, irreverently he supposed, as "doing the dirty work." Even in the earliest days of the Christian church, the apostles had figured out a way to hand off the housekeeping tasks by creating the deacon's order. Tradition dictated that deacons worked for free or, to put it more positively, for the love of God.

Deacon Mary was the one who collected toys to give away at Christmas, found spare shelter beds for their homeless regulars, "set the table" for communion, and put things away afterwards. Mary was truly the rock of their church, and Robert didn't know what he'd do without her. She was practical, too. His best loafers were soaked, while the galoshes peeking out from under her robe performed perfectly. Her civilian clothes were sensible, too, running to plaid blouses, crew-neck sweaters, and khaki skirts. Her pixie cut seemed impervious to the rain and wind.

Mary's job, once the hole was dug, was to bend down, remove the top from the box, turn it over and shake hard, making sure that Neola's earthly remains settled into their final resting place near her husband Fred's. No fancy urns were necessary or permitted, since the garden's occupants had all agreed (in advance, of course) that their dust would return directly to the dust to keep the lawn green for Easter egg hunts, animal blessings, and summer coffee hours.

Earlier in the day Henry had removed the top layer of turf, so the dirt should have yielded easily, given the water-saturated ground. However, Henry seemed to be having trouble. He retracted the shovel, took a breath and plunged it in with his right foot. The sharp crack of splitting wood emanated from the earth.

ca

Amidst the gasps and cries inspired by the cracking sound, Deacon Mary clutched the box containing Neola's ashes to her chest and stepped quickly out of Robert's way so that he could reach over to support Henry. The sexton had dropped the shovel and was hopping around on one leg, the other having been thrown into spasm by the sharp impact. The rest of the mourners had the appearance of a Greek chorus, alternately surging forward under their umbrellas to peer at the point of impact, then scooting backward to escape whatever dark forces the earth might release. Their rational minds must realize that the obstacle was benign, but Mary knew that their irrational minds were conjuring up a century-old coffin.

Neola's family seemed to share this vision and was hopping up and down along with Henry. Seeing a need for her pastoral skills, Mary stepped sideways through the group until she reached them. She remembered when Neola's daughter Audrey had faithfully attended Grace church with her parents, even after her early first marriage. However, the almost hysterical woman in front of her was a very different Audrey. She'd have to find out what had happened.

Right now she had a more pressing concern. Only five feet tall herself, she knew it would be difficult to herd Audrey and her husband off to the side while at the same time juggling the box.

She spied a white robe at the other edge of the crowd and barked, "Daniel, come here and hold Neola!" To the young organist's *Who, me?* look peeking through his long, curly mop, she responded with a *Yes, you!* look of her own. In a minute he was at her side, gingerly accepting the handoff.

"Now, just calm down, everyone!" Father Robert, having ensured that both of Henry's legs were on firm ground, was facing off the group, which by now had grown in size as clients emerging from the food bank located in the church basement stopped to stare. Mary noticed that Raymond, the police officer who provided off-duty security at the food bank, was among them. She signaled to him by leaping up and down and waving over the crowd, and was relieved to see him moving toward the burial site.

Father Robert and Raymond conferred for a minute, and then gestured to Henry, who nodded a little uncertainly, shook his leg out, and resumed his position. This time he moved the shovel a foot back from the original cut and pushed it in carefully. Mary realized that they planned to unearth the obstacle before planting Neola's ashes and explained to Neola's daughter and son-in-law that there'd be a short delay. Henry seemed to be meeting no resistance and continued, making a circle. The watchers stood by in silence, but persisted in bending forward slightly with each push and backward as the shovel came out.

Neola's daughter, Audrey, on the other hand, cringed each time the shovel went in, and began muttering a rambling prayer. "Protect us, Lord, from the dark forces that have invaded Mother's resting place. Help us remove Mother and Daddy's ashes from this evil spot to one which your Holy Spirit blesses." She suddenly turned to Mary, demanding, "Give me my mother's ashes!"

Mary held out her empty hands while scanning the crowd. Where had Daniel gone?

ଓଃ

The obstacle, once unearthed, proved to be the size and shape of a wine crate. It *was* a wine crate, Robert Vickers realized. As a matter of fact, he told Raymond, the security officer, it was the same type of crate that held the sweet wine used by Grace Church for communion services. The top looked to have been removed and then crudely re-nailed.

"Good job, Henry! Now go to the tool closet and bring back a crowbar," he ordered.

While they were waiting, the priest noticed that the number of food bank clients and other spectators had swelled and were spilling into the street. A man in a turban jostled against another sporting a suit and fedora. A woman wearing a long navy blue dress and veil was offering her potatoes to a Hawaiian-shirted fellow in exchange for his rice.

The babble of many languages rose on the rainy breeze, lending the scene the air of a modern-day Pentecost. All that was missing was the dove, although there were plenty of pigeons underfoot, hoping for a handout. Robert was not surprised to see the tall figure of Clare, known to all as the Pigeon Lady, among the crowd, swathed head to foot in a hooded brown robe.

Wherever she went, the pigeons followed, even though the Health Officer had persuaded her to stop feeding them. Robert also spotted Marjory, Clare's caretaker, standing nearby and shaking her head as if to say, "What can I do?" Clare's arms were outstretched, as if to bless them all, bird and human alike.

A baby-blue police cruiser poked its way up the street through the crowd. The vehicle stopped midstream, and then its door pushed open against the surrounding bodies. A curly blonde head and blue-clad torso emerged and loomed over the crowd. The patrol officer waded toward Raymond and Father Vickers, using her broad shoulders to part the waters. Once on the other side, she eyed the pile of dirt, the hole in the ground and the split box, and asked Raymond, "Well, well, Officer Chen. Got funeral duty today?"

"Very funny, Officer Hitchcock," he replied, brown eyes meeting her baby blues. "What I've got is a big mess. Father Vickers here was trying to bury some remains when the gravedigger ran into this box."

Joyce Hitchcock glanced around the garden area. "This doesn't look like a graveyard to me."

Robert intervened. "It's a memorial garden, officer, consecrated for the purpose of interring the ashes of the deceased of this church. It's—oh, it doesn't matter—I want to find out what's inside this box. We were just getting ready to open it."

"But what if there's a body inside?" croaked Henry the sexton, crowbar at the ready. Realizing from the quizzical looks he was receiving that a wine box wasn't quite large enough for this purpose, he amended his question in a more forceful tone, "Well, what if there's a body *part* inside?"

This brought Neola's son-in-law to attention. He escaped from Deacon Mary's comforting grasp and poked his head into the circle, sputtering, "Look here, you … you … you've dis— diser— *dese*rated my mother-in-law's funeral.

14

Officers, I demand that you take some action!"

"We are taking some action, sir," Raymond answered. "We're going to open this box."

"Well, could you please do it," urged Joyce, "sooner rather than later? I'd like to get this crowd dispersed before the TV helicopters descend on us."

"TV?" shouted the son-in-law, attracting more of the crowd's attention. "Audrey," he shouted louder, "the TV helicopters are coming!"

CR

Robert removed a handkerchief from the hidden pocket in his robe and wiped his broad forehead. Of all the infernal things to happen right now, this took the cake. "NOW JUST CALM DOWN!" the frustrated Father exhorted, glaring at Neola's son-in-law. "If you're so worried about des-e-*cra*-tion, you'd be wise to put your lips together and serve as a SILENT, REVERENT witness to the opening of this box. Now, Henry, you may proceed."

It took only a minute for Henry to dislodge the loose nails. Everyone in the immediate vicinity leaned in yet again, and with a final *Craaack*, the top of the box came off, revealing its contents: a plastic container much like the one holding Neola's ashes and a pair of black patent-leather lace-up shoes with chunky heels. The laces were red, or had been. The items were a little the worse for wear, since dirt had sifted through the seams of the crate. The shoes were showing signs of mildew and the container was stained.

Henry stared bug-eyed at the sight. Then a sound like a big mouse would make came from the direction of the rhododendrons. Robert looked up to see his organist Daniel opening and closing his mouth, but was immediately distracted by the son-in-law shouting, "What's that box doing there? And those funny shoes with the red laces? Are Dad's ashes in that box? Is—?"

"Calm. Down. Sir," chorused Robert and officers Chu and Hitchcock.

As Robert looked up to confer with the officers over the next course of action, his eyes widened, and he broke away from the circle. Lucy Lawrence was holding her throat and gasping.

ର

"Lucy! Lucy! Are you all right?"

Lucy peered into Father Robert's eyes, made huge by the thick lenses of his glasses, which were two inches away from her face.

"I'm, I'm, I don't know … How could the shoes …?"

"What about the shoes?" he answered. "Never mind. Don't talk right now."

She felt herself being supported by Father and two of the onlookers "I'm fine, just a little lightheaded," she assured them in a sturdy voice she willed not to quaver. "Please don't hover! You've got more important things to attend to. I'll just go inside and have a cup of tea and a cookie."

Oh, darn, darn, blast and darn, she thought as she walked toward the parish hall. *Why did I blurt that out about the shoes? Maybe Father will forget. But what if he doesn't? What shall I say? I'll just say they reminded me of some shoes I need to pick up from the repair shop. Ridiculous! He'd see through that in a second. I'll think of something plausible as I drink my tea.*

ର

Officer Hitchcock called out, "Hey, Pastor, come over here. There are ashes in the container." She poked her finger around. "And look at this, Pastor, there's a few pieces of bone floating around in here."

Robert peered in, and commented, "That happens sometimes."

"It's a large box, and it's heavy." the officer said. "Maybe its two people's ashes."

"No," Robert said. "Cremains—that's the word they use—weigh between three and eight pounds, depending on the person's size."

Neola's son-in-law, who'd been peering over the officer's shoulder, turned and gagged.

"Officer," he spluttered, wiping his mouth, "you'll need to fill out a police report."

ଓ

Officer Hitchcock disagreed. "Now why should I take the trouble to file a report saying there's been ashes found in a graveyard? And these funny shoes with the red laces? Who'd want them?"

The son-in-law continued, "But—but whose are they? Why are they in our family's plot? Isn't that theft—of something?"

"Well," the officer replied, "I could look in the criminal code, but I doubt we'd find a category for theft of a piece of grass." As she finished speaking, her hand rose to the top of her police hat to keep it on. "And with this wind coming up, I think we should wrap up this service. Raymond, what do you think? Raymond?"

Raymond was staring across the lawn at the side entry to the church, where a stone was just then crashing onto the cement, spraying gray chips in every direction. It was about two feet square and six inches thick, a fine specimen of the local Wilkinson sandstone cladding the building.

The group, led by Neola's family, screamed at the sound and sight of flying chips and leapt back, even though the point of impact was at least twenty-five feet away. All heads turned up and scanned the façade to see if more stones were coming.

"Stay back, everyone," said Officer Hitchcock. I'll get some hazard tape out of my cruiser."

Henry, the sexton, pulled his gaze from the unearthed crate and piped up. "Don't bother. We have some left over from the last time a stone fell. What did I tell you?" he added, turning toward Robert.

୧

"Thank you, Henry, for letting everyone know." Robert turned to the officer. "That stone isn't part of the tower structure; it's a piece of the stone cladding. We've been doing spot repairs until we raise enough funds for a major restoration." The grout around it hasn't been redone in—let's see—a while."

"It's been ninety years!" shouted Henry.

Robert noticed what appeared to be dollar signs in the son-in-law's eyes as the man exclaimed, "We could sue, ah, you could be sued over this!" Mr. Miller stood up straight and removed his baseball cap. "I happen to know something about buildings. Hey you," he continued, nodding toward Henry. "Since it looks like this burial is over for now, come with me while I give this building the onceover. Then I'll report my findings to the, what's he called, Audrey?"

"He's called the Bishop," she answered. "And I'll tell you right now," she continued, setting her sights on Robert, "he should shut this place down. It's old and crumbly and dark and cold and the seats are uncomfortable." She looked at the motley crew surrounding them. "And God knows who just used the bathroom before you." She clasped her arms around her. "And after today, I never, ever, want to see this place again!"

Before Robert could protest, Mr. Miller and Henry were

off and Audrey was herding her children toward the parish hall and the refreshments.

Joyce took out a pad, made a note, and commented to Robert, "A real neat freak, huh?

"Now pastor, your church is in my patrol area and I expect to see that tape up until the powers that be in the city engineering office decide it can come down. Raymond, I say we let the pastor dispose of the ashes and other items however he wants while we clear up this crowd and get back to work."

ଔ

Lucy, still paused at the door of the parish hall, almost fainted again. Dispose of them? Impossible! Whose ashes were they? And why were the special shoes there? Even though it touched upon her deepest fears and regrets, she couldn't allow this mystery to go unsolved. She'd have to speak to Father and a few of the others. She resolved to do so quickly ... after a cookie and a cup of tea.

ଔ

Rick Chase, who'd arrived just as the crate was being unearthed and stood at the edge of the crowd throughout the rest of the proceedings, shook his head. No way was he going to meet the family now. They had lawsuit written all over them. And all these other people—like a mini-United Nations. He had no idea it was so busy here during the week, having only attended on Sundays and for evening vestry meetings.

It was definitely time for a talk with Glenn, his real-estate developer friend. This scene was 180 degrees from the ambience they'd planned for the *Church Square Development*. Two things were for sure: the food bank had to go and this so-called Memorial Garden needed to be enclosed by a tall, locked fence.

CR

Waving goodbye to Officer Hitchcock, Robert tried to wrap his brain around everything he needed to do. First was to track down his organist and retrieve Neola's ashes. They'd have to delay the internment, but they might as well go on with the reception. On his way to the church he saw Rick Chase, his vestry member, edging away from the throng. He seemed distinctly uncomfortable being jostled about by food bank clients and street people. Did he think the church grounds were quiet and pristine between his Sunday visits?

Of all the people to see the cladding stone come off the tower, Rick was the worst. Under ordinary circumstances he'd ask Rick to help with repair planning, since his vestry member was an engineer. But he was beginning to wonder if "repair" was what Rick had in mind.

Turning toward the church, Robert saw a flash of movement inside one of the tall rhododendrons surrounding the garden. He shouted, "Daniel! I see you hiding there. Come out now, and bring Neola with you!"

CR

Hours later, after everyone had left, Robert beckoned Deacon Mary to follow him to his office. The crate of ashes and shoes they'd unearthed in the Memorial Garden was in the middle of the floor. Robert was notorious for using the floor as a combination filing cabinet and staging area for stacks of paper, stray candlesticks, and other things no one knew what to do with.

"Mary," Robert said, once they were settled down, "There's something strange about Lucy Lawrence's reaction to all this. That remark she made about 'her shoes' doesn't make sense. And then she came up to me during the reception and almost begged me not to throw the ashes and shoes away. As if I'd do such a thing! I'd better go see her tomorrow."

Mary told Robert that she'd seen Lucy peppering the Daniel the organist with questions but hadn't been close enough to hear what was being said. Daniel had looked bewildered, as usual. That curly-headed boy sure could play the organ, but his social skills were non-existent. However, after a minute, she told Robert, he'd become quite animated, bobbing his head every which-way and rising up and down on his toes.

Robert, now standing and moving piles of paper around with his feet, asked, "When exactly did the landscapers remove that turf from the garden? Was it after Neola's husband died?"

"Not long after," Mary replied. "Let's see ... it was a year ago last October. They wanted to put down the new turf in the fall. I do know the landscaper got an unlisted number after the umpteenth angry phone call asking what he'd done with grandpa's ashes."

The laughing pair looked up to see Henry the sexton standing in the doorway holding a large ring of keys. A red hunting hat completed his steel-gray ensemble.

"It's time to lock up," the sexton announced. I've shooed everyone away and turned out all the lights 'cept this one. Out you go. I ain't got all night."

Robert stood up and moved toward the door, stopping a foot away from Henry. Still sitting in her chair, Mary widened her eyes in anticipation of the sparks that would fly. Robert elongated his neck to its limit so that he could speak from a bit higher vantage point.

"We'll be on our way shortly," he said to Henry, "but first I want a report on your building tour with Neola's son in law. I could have used your help at that point in the proceedings, but off you went to give aid and comfort to a guy who hates us and everything we stand for."

Crouching like a cornered dog, Henry barked out an answer. "That ain't true! I wasn't going to let him poke around without someone to keep an eye on him!" Straightening up, Henry went on, "And a good thing, too, because I found out what his familiarity with buildings consists of. He works for an extermination company, that's what! Don't worry, I didn't show him any of the other cracks or missing stones. I led him right to that blackberry patch on the south corner. Left him there to communicate with the rats and other critters."

Robert raised his hands and said, "I give up, Henry. I'll just have to go on faith that you have the church's best interests at heart. Now let's make our exit."

Chapter 2

Deacon Mary Martin arrived home fifteen minutes later, exhausted from her eventful day. She turned off the engine of her Mini-Cooper—purchased because its seat was perfectly designed for her mini-stature—and slumped back, resting for a moment in the glow of the brightly lit garage. What a good idea it had been for her and Joe to move to this cozy downtown condo with its convenient parking and other amenities.

Her favorite amenity was the little camera that let them screen visitors. At the big corner house near the church, they'd been besieged at all hours by people seeking handouts. Word that she was a soft touch seemed to have spread throughout the city.

Her day wasn't over yet. There was dinner to make, unless Joe had cooked something. He'd want to know all about the excitement at the church. Her brief phone call wouldn't have satisfied him.

Since retiring as an insurance investigator last year, Joe had taken more interest in her job. He chauffeured her in the middle of the night to the emergency room to visit sick parishioners and excelled at waylaying the occasional overenthusiastic seeker of help who was off her meds or the worse for drink.

Joe's job investigating suspicious fires and thefts had

made him suspicious of everyone, while her deacon's position came with a pair of rose-colored glasses. She smiled, remembering the spectacular arguments they'd had over her more innovative plans, like the time she wanted supply the local panhandlers with coffee and donuts to sell to commuters at the freeway exits.

She got out of the car and headed to the elevator. After they ate, she'd begin calling her shut-ins, the ones too ill or disabled to attend church regularly. Despite visiting them frequently, somehow she'd also wound up calling them all every night. It had started when Rose at Heritage House had an anxiety attack and begged Mary to call at bedtime to say a prayer. One night had turned into two in a row, then ten, and then nightly. Of course Rose had bragged to Agnes and Helen that Deacon Mary prayed with her *every night*, so she'd had to call them, too. Then the dears had called their friends at West Shore Manor. The next thing you knew she'd be tucking them all into bed.

"Hi, sweetie," she called out. "Is that macaroni dinner I smell? The kind that comes in a box with the powdered cheese? What a prince you are!"

"Why thank you, darling. My pleasure to serve you," a voice answered from the kitchen. She hurried down the hallway and gazed appreciatively at her much taller husband, with his crinkly eyes and salt-and-pepper crew cut, sitting ramrod straight at the kitchen table.

As she wolfed down the macaroni, Mary told Joe about finding the mysterious box and the aftermath. Against all odds, with a few discreet hints about the extra expense involved in arranging an alternate location, she'd managed to convince Neola's daughter Audrey to delay, not cancel, the internment. Upon reflection, she'd realized that Audrey's fragile mental state at the service was understandable.

Audrey had been the shy, protected only-child of a Type A executive father and a flamboyant socialite mother. She'd lived in their shadows until escaping into a disastrous marriage at age twenty-one. After the divorce was final five years later, she'd moved back home with her two children. Discreet interrogation of a few family friends at the reception revealed that Audrey had bolted again a few years ago to marry Mark Miller, a man she'd met at a singles' mixer. Soon she'd been enjoying the security and predictability of a life centered around her new church community in the suburbs.

Drying the dishes as Joe washed, Mary remarked that Father Robert had acquitted himself handsomely at the reception, greeting everyone by name in his raspy baritone, inviting the food bank clients to join the party, and then soliciting reminiscences about their departed friend. Audrey had even relaxed a bit and surprised everyone by recounting the time her mother had snatched a designer dress out of another woman's hands at a Frederick and Nelson's sale. The original group of elderly mourners was delighted to be part of what was amounting to a festive wake. Neola would have approved of her sendoff, especially the colorful attire of the guests from the food bank. The two police officers had stayed on for the reception, too. "I think Joyce and Raymond might end up as a twosome, even though she could fit him in her little pocket," Mary told Joe.

Moving to the living room, they settled into their respective recliners. Joe had a few questions of his own. "When exactly did the landscapers remove that turf from the garden? Was it after Neola's husband died?"

"Robert asked the same question. Not long after," Mary replied. "Let's see … a year ago last October. They wanted to put down the new turf in the fall. I do know the landscaper got an unlisted number after the umpteenth angry phone call asking what he'd done with grandpa's ashes."

Joe chuckled, even though he'd heard this story before. "Did the grass over Neola and Fred's plot look any different from the rest, as if it had been disturbed?"

"Now Joe, you know I'd never notice something like that. I do know that the spot is at one end of the lawn, right next to that big rhododendron that's dyi—"

"Dying? Whoever planted that crate could have dug next to the bush and disturbed the roots. And those ashes, you're sure they're human?"

"Well, Sweetness, I suppose they could have belonged to a hamster." Ignoring Joe's narrowed eyes, she continued, "I guess Robert will be trying to find out. Do you know if it's possible to identify someone by their ashes or the little bits of bone—you know, by their DNA or something?"

"I don't think so," Joe answered. But just to make sure, I'll make a few calls tomorrow.

"But you know," he continued, "the biggest problem the church has right now is that blasted bell tower. Robert just can't continue to send Henry up a ladder to replace the grout. For one thing, that old codger doesn't know what he's doing, and for another, the whole tower needs to be rebuilt from the ground up. I'd better sign on as a consultant and find Robert a decent engineer."

"That's generous of you, dear," said Mary, heading to make her phone calls, "but I want to know why someone would bury a crate full of ashes and shoes in the Memorial Garden. And was it a coincidence that the rock crashed down right afterwards? Maybe Neola's daughter was right and there are dark forces at work."

"I knew your gift for flights of fancy would appear sooner or later, dear," Joe commented. "Between the two of us, we might just solve this little mystery."

 С

Robert scuffed the toes of his shoes against the sidewalk as he approached the rectory. He'd had this bad habit since childhood. His dreamy small self had always lagged behind, kicking leaves and stones—or imaginary objects if real ones were unavailable. It helped him think, and he needed help now.

After Mary had left for home, while Henry made one last check of the building, he'd sat in his swivel chair staring at the box of ashes—at one time a human being with a unique and precious life. Only prayer could address moments such as these—moments of doubt, sadness, and quiet longing to know the unknowable. He meditated on the box and its contents as if it were a candle, or an icon. Then he sat up, refreshed, and turned his mind to more practical matters.

Despite the indifference of the police, Robert needed to know how the crate and its contents had come to rest in the garden, and if possible, the identity of the human being whose life had ended this way. Was the death connected to the church in some way? His intuition and common sense told him yes.

He might as well gather a bit more information before going to bed. Turning into the rectory walkway, he saw with satisfaction that Daniel's light was on in the upstairs window. Since the organist had moved into one of the spare bedrooms, Robert had welcomed the extra lighted window at night. He'd also welcomed Daniel's company in the overly spacious lodgings built in the early 1900s for a large clerical family. Except when hosting the occasional ministry student or guest preacher, Robert had spent his nights alone.

His first and only marriage had ended thirty years ago, soon after he graduated from seminary. Sandy hadn't fancied juggling two careers at once and had chosen medicine over minister's wife. Since then, he'd had several discreet relationships, all but one with women who wanted nothing to do with organized (or unorganized) religion. The one he hoped would lead to marriage had ended abysmally soon before he came to Grace Church.

Daniel had meant for his stay at the rectory to be

temporary until he found a place of his own. However, Robert sensed that the young man welcomed the company as much as he did.

Not that they spoke much. He'd tried, but Daniel LaSalle was the strangest conversationalist he'd ever met. Not shy, exactly. He could speak clearly and even forcefully while conducting the choir and waxed eloquent when discussing the great organists. Off stage, however, his communication consisted mostly of head movements, with an occasional rambling monologue trailing off into nowhere.

Amazingly enough, it sufficed. It was possible to carry on a conversation with Daniel if you didn't mind doing most of the talking and keeping tight control of the subject matter. The young man opened his hazel eyes wide and nodded vigorously to express agreement. A big "oh" of the mouth plus bigger eyes meant surprise, and a slant of the eyebrows peeking through his brown curls screamed disdain when combined with a certain curl of the lip. Robert was reminded of the little faces people used to decorate their emails.

However, he wasn't sure Daniel's repertoire would be up to the questions he meant to put to him tonight. Why had the musician been so surprised to see that box and those shoes? They'd surely been buried long before he'd been hired. And what had he and Lucy discussed so intently at the reception? Daniel's head had been moving so much, and in so many different directions, it brought to mind one of those toys with springs for a neck.

But Robert was skilled at dragging information out of reluctant people. He'd tackle Daniel tonight, and then beard Lucy in her den first thing in the morning.

To avoid stubbing his toe on the rectory's old-fashioned front door stoop, he'd trained himself to lift up his foot after unlocking the door. It worked unless he was distracted. His loud "God Bless It!" as he stubbed his toe echoed through the rectory, as did the sound of the massive oak door slamming against the entry wall.

The faint light at the top of the stairs went dark almost simultaneously. After closing and locking the door and putting the hall rug to rights, Robert limped up the stairs, not to be denied enlightenment on the subject of the shiny shoes.

"Open up, Daniel; I know you're in there and I know you're awake."

The tall, paneled door opened into the darkness.

"Where are you, man? Turn on the light!"

A hand, presumably Daniel's, appeared in front of him and moved to the right. In a few seconds the room was flooded with harsh light from the bare ceiling bulb. Robert made a mental note to replace the fixture as he addressed Daniel, "Now, come out from the corner!"

"Oh. Father. Sorry. I'm, ah, a little jumpy tonight."

"Jumpy? God knows, we should all be jumpy after today's events. Sit down, son. We need to talk."

Daniel nodded and sat on the edge of the tightly made bed. Robert took the stool belonging to the massive upright piano taking up most of the room. He shuddered, remembering the contortions involved in getting the beast up the narrow stairway, through the narrow door and into the small room. He was facing the room's only decoration, a life-sized poster of a fuzzy white baby penguin. Daniel had a thing about penguins.

"Now tell me what you know about the shoes in that crate and why you seemed so surprised and what Lucy was asking you and why you've been avoiding me?"

Daniel lowered his head and nodded. "In that order?"

"In whatever order it takes to get you to talk."

"Yes. Well. Um, ah … Yes."

Robert waited. He was used to these preliminaries and knew enough not to interrupt.

"Yes. Yes! The shoes. Well, I suppose you've never noticed, because my shoes are hidden underneath the organ, and I do remove them immediately after service is over because they mustn't be scuffed, and they're expensive. They have to be special-ordered, and there are only a few companies that make them. Unless you want to buy them from Capezio or one of the other dance suppliers. But those are, are … derivative, and I want to support the profession."

Robert was beginning to get used to his organist's habit of talking round and round a subject.

"So organ players need special shoes for some reason when they're playing. Probably having to do with all that foot pumping."

Daniel nodded enthusiastically.

Encouraged, Robert carried on, "And the shoes in that crate, they were that type of shoe?"

More nodding.

"Are they your shoes?"

Daniel caught himself mid-nod and shook his head.

"Oh, no. For one thing, they're too big. Old fashioned, too. Patent leather. The upper parts stick to each other when you're moving between pedals. You have to use baby powder on them. That's messy."

"Very enlightening," Robert said. "The shoes of an organist—either an old-fashioned organist or an old organist. Either new old-fashioned shoes or old old-fashioned shoes. How about the red laces?"

Daniel frowned and said, "Why would someone substitute red laces for the black ones that come with the shoes? Why? Hmm. Why? Oh! I think I know.

"Some of the younger, I mean younger than me, classical musicians … their managers are promoting them like rock stars. They wear non-traditional clothes, um, bright colors, dresses that show, ah," Daniel's hand waved vaguely toward his chest, "and lots of rings and necklaces and things."

Daniel paused. Robert waited for him to continue, "Um. Well, I suppose organists could wear red laces if they wanted that kind of attention. But usually it's the violinists and opera singers. Our profession is pretty stuffy."

"Thank you, Dan. Now tell me, what did Lucy Lawrence want to know?"

"Pretty much the same thing, except she knew what kind of shoes they are because her brother's a famous organist. He played with the symphony here, and still does some concerts."

Now Robert's head went up and down. "I'd forgotten she told me that. So what else did she want to know?"

"Um, she wanted to know if those shoes could belong to a female. I told her they were a little large, but both men and women use the lace-ups. Of course the women can wear pumps, like the ones Dorothy wore in the *Wizard of Oz*. Only not red and sparkly. And organ pumps have a strap across the middle so they won't fall off."

"But these had red laces. Did Lucy wonder why?"

Head shake.

"No? Well *I* wonder why, and I think she *knows* why. I'm going to ask her tomorrow."

❧

Daniel hadn't answered all his questions, but it was all Robert could expect for now, he thought, as he walked up the stairs to his attic bedroom. When he'd arrived at the parish five years before, the top floor was filled with 100 years of cast-offs, and not only from its previous rectors and their families. There were broken pews from the church, old typewriters and mimeo machines from the office, tiny chairs from the Sunday school, wine-stained linen from the sacristy, and even extra cases of provisions from the food bank. Before cleaning it out he called the Diocesan historian, who found quite a bit to interest him.

Convincing the church old-timers that twenty-five copies of the church directory circa 1945 and the faux mahogany settee with horsehair upholstery donated by Mrs.

31

Belmont's grandmother were not sacred objects was a titanic struggle that almost lost him his job.

After succeeding in clearing out the space—partly by giving in and finding new hidey holes for the most fiercely fought-over items—he'd begun renovation. Now he had a skylight over his bed and a casement window with a spectacular view of the city. The smell of 100–year-old fir perfumed the air. The walls were ringed with shelves containing books inappropriate for the church's library. His original collection of every single *Mad Magazine* and every Zane Grey western had pride of place. Robert did his best thinking up here.

Before turning off the bedside light, he picked up the book he often turned to for inspiration. The slender paperback with the bizarre title, *Parson McFright: Short Stories for Harried Churchmen,* had been written by a minster one generation ahead of him, a fellow by the name of Allan Whitman. The thick glasses and balding head of the harried churchman on the cover resembled his own.

Robert, who had picked it up for nothing from the cast-off pile at church headquarters, soon found that Parson McFright—although operating in the 1960s—was faced with conundrums similar to his, like the time they both forgot their sermon text at the rectory and had to give an impromptu homily on the Holy Trinity.

Although the stories never involved an unidentified box of ashes, they did touch upon the myriad ways parishioners have of holding onto secrets. After a few minutes, however, he was fast asleep, the book rising and falling on his chest.

Chapter 3

At 7:30 Wednesday morning, Lucy Lawrence was settled in the living room reading from her prayer book. A small group met daily at the church to say these same prayers, called the "Morning Office," but she preferred to say them in solitude. All over the world, men and women began their days by reading the ancient words of the psalms and gospels. The Confession of Sin especially consoled her: "Almighty and most merciful Father, we have erred and strayed from thy ways like lost sheep, we have followed too much the devices and desires of our own hearts." She ended with a period of meditation and a few Yoga poses for good measure.

The residents of Heritage House knew better than to disturb her between 7:30 and 8:30. Even the cats, satisfied that they'd eaten and visited with her over her first cup of coffee, stayed in the bedroom. The kitties associated the pungent smell of grinding beans with breakfast, which they ate from two bowls placed at either end of Lucy's tiny galley kitchen. After eating and drinking heartily, Stella and Luna played a game of kitty hockey with the extra kibbles, their paws serving as sticks. From time to time they stopped to scoop up water from their bowls with their paws to drip it on their linoleum rink. Lucy wandered sleepily though the game like an errant goalie, crunching as she went.

Now she was in the middle of reading Psalm 95 ("The

sea is his for he made it, and his hands have molded the dry land") when the doorbell rang. Irritation replaced the joy accorded by the majestic phrases.

Lucy closed her prayer book, urged reluctant knees to bring her to her feet, and approached the front door. The bell sounded loudly again in her ear. The cats followed in her wake, intrigued as always by a change in routine.

She turned the lock and opened the door. "Father, what are you doing out so early?"

Seeing the red prayer book in her hand, Robert answered, "Lucy, I'm sorry for interrupting your devotions, but I have to be at the bishop's office at nine to give him a heads-up on yesterday's discovery. That's what I want to talk to you about."

"Come in, then," she answered, "but I'm afraid you're mistaken if you think I have any relevant information."

Lucy followed him into the compact living room, where the cats had positioned themselves in front of the couch. She smiled as Stella, watched intently by Luna, pushed her nose into the cuffs of Robert's pants. From previous experience, they knew that pant creases harbored goodies such as stray acorns. Once, to their delight, a live grasshopper had hopped out and kept them (and Lucy) amused for hours.

Robert was a good sport. "Are you finished, cats? Can I sit down now?"

To Lucy's offer of coffee he answered, "I'd love some, but after we're finished talking. Now Lucy, Daniel reminded me that your brother is quite a famous organist. And of course you know that the shoes in the crate belonged to an organist. I'm certainly not suggesting that your brother was in any way involved, but you're familiar with the profession and the circles that organists move in. I'd love your help in getting to the bottom of this."

He leaned back, clasping his knee. "But first I have to ask why your reaction was so strong yesterday, and why you referred to them as 'her shoes.' I suspected your falling-out with your brother was serious when he stopped attending Grace Church. Was it the memory of those events that upset you?"

A tear trickled slowly down Lucy's cheek, and the cats jumped up to snuggle against her.

"Father Robert, believe me, I have no idea why the shoes were buried there." She might as well tell him. "It wasn't my brother I was thinking of; it was his daughter Lisa, my niece. She has—or had—a pair of shoes resembling the ones in the box. Their laces were also red."

"No wonder you were so shocked," Robert said. "Could you start from the beginning? Don't worry about the time. The Bishop can wait."

"Not without my second cup of coffee."

As they settled down again with their cups, Robert said, "I met your brother and Lisa when I first came to Grace Parish, but I haven't seen them in a long while."

Lucy answered, "Remember when I came to see you a year ago and I was in such a state? I explained then that my brother had caused a breach between my niece and me. Besides him, she's my only living family. You assured me that the rift would heal with time. Well, it hasn't."

"Why haven't you told me?" Robert sputtered, and then paused. "No, why didn't I ask? Forgive me, Lucy."

"Forgiven. I've been nursing my hurt in silence, a bad habit I've developed over the years. Thomas is fifteen years younger than I. He married rather late because his early career as a concert organist involved a lot of travel. He met his wife Sue when she interviewed him for a music publication. They had one daughter, Lisa."

Lucy paused for a minute while the cats re-settled themselves on her lap. "Thomas has always been a perfectionist, and he's high-strung as well. He started Lisa on a keyboard at age three and had her at the organ as soon as she could reach the pedals. She's been giving recitals on both the piano and organ since she was nine.

"Sadly, Sue died when Lisa was ten," she continued. "She'd managed to keep some balance in Lisa's life, making sure she had a normal childhood involving school, friends and sports. That changed after her death. Thomas insisted that Lisa spend all her time outside of school at her music."

"That must have been hard on a young girl," Robert murmured. "Had you moved from Delaware to Seattle yet?"

Lucy shooed the cats away, stood and went to the south facing window, which provided a view of the Grace Church spire.

"No, but I'd put my dental practice up for sale after Sue died, and when it sold, I came west. I was eager to become involved in my niece's life, I suppose for my sake as much as hers. As you know, I don't have children of my own."

She turned away from the window.

"At first Thomas appreciated my involvement and willingness to take the girl shopping and out to lunch, the usual things aunts do."

She went to the bookshelf and picked up a picture. "For her eleventh birthday, I gave Lisa her first grownup pair of organ shoes. They were patent-leather lace-ups, like the ones unearthed yesterday in the crate. I included the red laces as a hint that she shouldn't take her music too seriously." She brought the picture over to Robert, who smiled.

"Here we are at her birthday dinner," she continued. "I'll never forget how proudly she wore them, complete with red laces, at church with me the next Sunday, even though the shoes are supposed to be reserved for the actual playing of the organ.

"As you might expect, Thomas wasn't pleased at what he termed my 'frivolity,' and forbade Lisa from wearing the red laces in public. Worse, he began forbidding any activity that would take Lisa away from her music."

She glanced at her watch. "You really will be late. I'm

almost done. A year and a half ago, I planned an excursion to San Diego during Lisa's spring break. She was especially looking forward to seeing the zoo and swimming in the ocean. But it meant that she would miss two rehearsals for an upcoming performance, so Thomas refused to let her go.

"It was heartbreaking to see her so torn between loyalty to her father and her desire to have a few days off from her strict schedule. That started the rift between us. Thomas probably didn't mean to, but his disapproval of me encouraged Lisa to take sides. She began refusing my offers to go to the movies, shopping, the things she'd loved to do. The more I tried to intervene, the more upset Thomas got, and after one final ugly confrontation, I decided to withdraw for the girl's sake. Other than calling on their birthdays, I've had no contact with either one." She turned away and choked, "not even at Christmas."

Robert was quiet.

"What are you thinking?" she asked after a moment. "Don't worry about my sensibilities."

He answered, "Your story breaks my heart. You've shown amazing fortitude by staying in Seattle and creating a productive life in spite of what's happened. I'll be praying for a reconciliation."

He stood up. "I'd better be off to wedge myself into the Bishop's hyperactive schedule."

Pausing, he added, "Isn't it interesting that the shoes found in that crate are just like your niece's? That they appear to have been buried just before your falling out with your brother … although I certainly hadn't guessed that something of that nature had occurred."

Lucy felt a thunderclap in her brain as she tried to suppress her suspicion that the two events might be linked.

"Father Robert, my mind's in a whirl," she said. "This has to be a coincidence, but I know I won't be able to let it rest until it is resolved."

Robert was smacking the side of his head with his left hand. "Why do I say these things! You'd think I was a boy detective instead of a supposedly mature priest. Sorry again, Lucy."

Lucy grinned. "If I come up with any other ideas, I'll let you know. Once thing I do know. It's time for me to reach out to my niece again, and, I suppose, to Thomas, too. Holding a grudge doesn't suit me."

Robert nodded. "That takes humility, and courage. And love. Good for you. Let me know how it goes. Oh, and one more thing. What did Daniel tell you yesterday at the funeral reception? He seemed agitated, more so than circumstances seemed to warrant."

"I imagine you've asked him the same question about my conversation with him," Lucy commented dryly. "He told me that the shoes seemed to be quite old, not so much scuffed and dirty as plain old-fashioned. The label, if there is one, might provide more information. That was all, other than his not knowing why the laces were red. You're right, though; he seemed less anxious than excited."

Robert looked up toward the ceiling, signaling that he was deep in thought. "I think I'll ask Deacon Mary to talk to him next. He seems to enjoy her motherly presence. So far as I know, Daniel doesn't have any relatives or friends nearby, although he's ducked that question, too. Now I'd better get going so I can catch the Bishop before *he* ducks out for an early lunch."

Lucy and the cats saw him out, and then returned to the living room. Lucy looked out the window for a moment, then sat down, picked up her book and resumed reading Morning Prayer.

The north-south Interstate Highway bisecting Seattle is

slightly elevated over the city center, leaving a no-man's land of concrete pillars, pavement, and city cross streets underneath. The right-of-way under the freeway is state property; however, the city and state seem equally uninterested in maintaining and policing the area. Another group has filled the vacuum.

CR

The morning after Neola's funeral service and her non-internment in the Memorial Garden, Deacon Mary Martin drove under the freeway on her way up the hill to Grace Church. She stopped at the light, pressed the button to roll down the car window, and greeted Lester, their churchyard camper, at the Northbound Freeway entrance. Today he was holding a hand-lettered sign that read, *Will work for food. God Bless.* Yesterday's sign had proclaimed, *Disabled veteran needs help. God Bless.*

"So you're working again today, Lester?" she asked. "Once your shift's over, come up to the church, and I'll give you a sack lunch and something more productive to do."

Lester leaned forward. "Sorry, Mother Mary, I can't leave, or else one of the other guys will take this corner. Thanks for the offer, though. I don't suppose you have a dollar or two to spare?"

"Not today, Lester," she answered. "Now, listen. You'll want to be at church on Sunday. The Bishop's preaching."

"Oh, he ain't half as good as the Padre!" Lester replied, "but I bet there'll be a good spread after, so okay." The next second the expression on his weathered face turned hard and Mary pulled back into the car.

"Nah," he muttered. "That blasted pigeon lady will probably be there, flapping around, muscling in on my territory."

"*Your* territory?" Mary asked. "Don't tell me you've

started panhandling at the church, too."

"Not much," he answered. "Only if someone looks like a real bleeding-hearter. But she snaps them all up with that witch's robe and the pigeons sitting on her head. And then she runs out with her take and buys bird seed. Something's gotta be done."

"That's enough, Lester," Mary warned. "We're all God's children. Even you."

As Mary drove under the freeway and up the hill, she spotted some of the others who called this part of town home. They started the day at the food bank, took turns standing at the corners with their shared signs, did odd jobs here and there, and camped under the freeway at night.

She'd tried all sorts of things to help them, including staking the guys with donuts to sell at freeway entrances. They'd changed their signs to read. *Donuts for sale. God Bless.* After a shaky start, proceeds were good, and the commuters loved it, especially after the pastries were cellophane-wrapped.

But the guys didn't. They wanted to keep all the money they made without reimbursing her for the donuts. Then the Health Officer intervened. Her latest plan was to encourage more local businesses to employ them as day laborers.

Many of them were war veterans, and most were practicing alcoholics or addicts who weren't welcome at the shelters. There were also a few women, who held their own in this rough environment.

Some clung to a vestige of their childhood religious faith, and all had colorful biographies she never tired of hearing. Most of them, like Lester, called her Mother Mary, which amused her, since the face in her mirror, topped with its pixie haircut, looked more like a wrinkled Peter Pan's than the mystical Virgin's.

After parking, Mary walked the tree-lined half block to the church. Its stone-clad spire shone buttery yellow in the morning sun. How could something that seemed so solid be so close to falling over, she wondered.

Mary nearly ran into Henry as she entered the parish office. The short, wiry sexton was wrestling a noisy buffing machine over the entry hall.

"Henry!" she yelled, and then coughed as *eau de wet floor wax* shot up her nose.

Turning his head, he yelled back, "Whoa, there! Don't track up my clean floor!"

"How else can I get to the office?" she asked. "Can you turn that thing off for a minute?"

"Oh, all right, but I'm in a hurry. It's only four days until the Bishop's visit, and I need to touch up the paint in all the bathrooms."

"I doubt the Bishop will notice, but I'm sure it will look lovely." *If you liked pea green*, she thought.

"As you *may* recall," Henry answered, "the Bishop does a white glove inspection of the whole building when he comes. He's an ex-military man. Claims a shabby church doesn't attract the right kind of clientele. I've got to tidy up Father Robert's office, too. The Bishop will have a conniption fit if he trips over that box of ashes."

Mary asked, "How did you know the ashes are there?"

"I spied them there last night, that's how."

Mary narrowed her eyes. "You'd better check with him before first."

As an unpaid member of the parish staff—even one who was seminary-educated and wore a 'dog collar'—she really had no business ordering Henry around, but her husband Joe had urged her not to let anyone else touch the box of ashes and shoes. He'd given her three thick plastic evidence bags to place them in and a pair of white stretchy gloves to use for the transfer. She wondered what else her husband had squirreled away as mementos of his career as an insurance investigator.

Joe had also suggested that the items be locked away for now. She mustn't forget to tell Robert when he came back from the Bishop's office.

She asked Henry, "Do you know where Daniel is?" Robert had called her this morning with some questions to ask the organist. Mary didn't think an interrogation would work too well with Daniel, so she'd bought some cookies on the way in anticipation of a cozy chat in her office. She and Daniel got along well. Like everyone else, he viewed her as a mother figure and was beginning to relax in her presence.

Before Henry could answer, a blast of organ music announced Daniel's location.

"I reckon he's in the church," Henry answered. "I wish I could say I liked the organ, but after all these years it still sounds like a peacock screeching. When Tim was here—that's two organists back—he used to make a noise like a trumpet for me. Now *that's* music!"

"That was before my time. I'll see you later," Mary said, as she headed through the passage connecting the parish office to the church.

Daniel had begun a different piece, much softer, that was sending waves of melancholy through the sanctuary. Approaching from the side, she noticed that the organist was dressed in black—from his shoes to his curly mop. The only exception was the white outline of a penguin on the back of his T-shirt. His usual uniform was a shabby green cable knit sweater and tan pants two sizes too large.

Mary stopped to listen for a minute, and then approached the console.

"That's lovely. What is it?"

"Oh! Ms. Mary!" Daniel jerked his hands off the organ keys, creating a cacophony of noise. "I didn't know you were … This? It's nothing, just … a motet I learned as a student."

"It sounds like something for a funeral. What's it called?"

"Oh, no, not a funeral," Daniel answered. "It's much more appropriate for a requiem Eucharist, except that requiems aren't performed much anymore." He patted the keys lightly. "Well, I guess it could be played at a funeral, given the lyrics—they're by Longfellow. He was a poet, not a lyricist."

Mary nodded.

Daniel continued, "Except there usually isn't a choir at a funeral. This has six parts. Our choir can hardly manage four. I suppose it could be played as an interlude, or possibly a prelude, or even a postlude—

"What's its name, Daniel?"

"Its name? Oh. Well, the name of the poem is 'The Dead,' but that's, ah, blunt. Most people refer to it by its first line. That's what Healey Willan titled it when he set it to music. In 1917."

After waiting for ten seconds, Mary asked, "And that first line would be—?"

"The first line, yes." Daniel looked away toward the rose window above the altar.

She waited.

"How they so softly rest," he murmured, continuing,

> All they the holy ones
> Unto whose dwelling Place
> Now doth my soul draw near.

He glanced at her. "There's more. I can give you a copy later but I have to go now."

"Lovely, Daniel, and so sad. Come by my office for a minute. I've got a new picture of my grandkids to show you. And some of that tea the monks make. And some cookies." If she didn't watch out she'd soon be speaking like him.

"Well, just for a minute," he answered. "I'm very busy. Lots to do. Planning for Pentecost."

"Pentecost isn't for three months," she reminded him.

"Three months is nothing to musicians," he answered. "I'm also planning for next Advent and Christmas. And the Bishop's coming this Sunday. Father Robert said he—the Bishop—wants contemporary music. To attract young families with kids."

He looked around before saying, "I can't. We musicians call it happy-clappy music. I can't. I won't. Besides, there was nothing like that in our music files. I found an Anthem written in 1980. That's as contemporary as I can manage."

A minute later, Mary was walking quietly beside him toward the parish hall. It was nice to be just a little shorter than someone, rather than a lot shorter. And she'd just thought of a new line of inquiry.

As they passed the secretary's desk outside Robert's office, she spied Henry. He began talking before she had a chance to admonish him again.

"Seems like I have to do everything around here! Every day I spend my first hour answering the phone until Marion comes at the fancy hour of nine."

Mary countered, "Yes, and she often stays until six or seven answering that phone and cleaning up water from the sink that likes to overflow the minute you leave at four."

Giving Henry one final, stern look, she corralled Daniel, who was sidling toward the piano in the parish hall.

After getting the organist settled with his tea in the overstuffed chair, she sank gratefully into the cushions of the matching couch, which made the space feel more like a living room than an office. Although it would be nice for Robert if he had a junior priest to help with the parish's many services, she felt fortunate to lay claim to the office marked "curate." The space came in especially handy at Christmas when she collected mountains of gifts for stranded seamen, homeless kids and immigrant families.

"Whew! My knees are still shaky from all the jumping up and down I did yesterday. What do you make of it, Dan?"

"*It?*"

"Yes, *it*. Finding the crate, and the shoes, and the ashes."

"Um. I don't know. Except that … at the church where I did my organ internship, a Lutheran church … somber, heavy music, 'A Mighty Fortress is Our God' and such …."

"Where was it located?"

"The music? Oh, you mean the church. Um, nowhere. I mean, it was somewhere, but it doesn't matter. Just a place."

"Now Daniel," she answered, "why wouldn't you want to say where you've worked? Besides, I could look it up on your résumé if I wanted."

"My résumé? Oh! I forgot. Anyway, I don't like to dwell too much on … in … *on* the past. I'm a future-oriented person, a good quality in a musician. I plan. In my head, all the time. That's why I sometimes seem a little … Well, Father has told me I'm spacey, although that's not the word I'd use." He took a third cookie.

"It's good enough," said Mary. "Anyway, we digress. You were telling me about something similar that happened at a Lutheran church. Before you go any further, are we about to stray off point again?"

"There will be a point. At the end. You see, the pastor there … they call them pastors, not priests. In the Lutheran church."

"I know that, dear."

"Anyway, he, the pastor, discovered ten urns full of ashes in an old safe, and nobody knew whose they were. We had one big memorial service for them. An anonymous memorial service. I played … I played … I—"

"Why, Daniel, you're crying!" Mary reached out her hand in sympathy, knowing better than to pat or hug him.

"It's nothing," he mumbled, looking at the floor. As

Mary watched and waited, his head slowly rose, and his blue eyes turned steely as they locked onto hers.

"Yes it is. It *is* something! I'll tell you. My father. My *real* father, not my stepfather. My real father was an organist, or *is* one, if he's still alive. I only knew him until I was five, when he left.

"He was gay. Mom told me when I was twelve. In the closet, but they found out somehow. At the church where he worked. They fired him. My mother wanted him to stay with us, even knowing he was gay. He said he loved us but had to leave anyway. That was twenty years ago, and we never saw him again. He left his favorite organ shoes behind. The ones I wear."

Daniel took a long sip of tea and continued, "The piece I was playing in church ... It's the same piece I played at the anonymous funeral. My dad's favorite. 'How They So Softly Rest.' "

"Thank you for telling me," Mary murmured.

"I'm tired of not having a past," Daniel said. "I *do* have a past, and my dad was a great organist. Everyone said so."

"And you've inherited his gifts," Mary answered. "He'd be proud of you. And now we've found the remains of someone who probably was also an organist. Let's do what we can to find out who that organist was."

After a brief pause, Daniel answered, "All right. The shoes in the box seem to be, uh, antiques. Made in the 1940s or maybe the 50s. They're very ... I think it's called elegant. I'll do some research." He paused again, longer this time. "And then I'm going to try to find my dad."

Mary smiled and wiped away a tear. "Daniel, that's a wonderful plan. Now, what do you know about your predecessors here at Grace Church?"

☙

Robert Vickers paused to adjust his clerical collar and slick down his fringe of salt and pepper hair. Drawing himself up to his full 5'10," he opened the door to Diocesan House, the Bishop's office.

The woman sitting behind the reception desk looked up and smiled. "Why, Father Vickers. How delightful to see you!"

"My sentiments exactly, Molly," Robert replied, handing her a multicolored bunch of tulips. His jaw dropped open and stayed that way as he surveyed her curvy figure, showcased in a tomato-red suit nipped in at the waist. The sunlight entering from the room's tall window burnished her wavy auburn hair. The scent of her lilac cologne floated into his nostrils.

"Earth to Robert," she chuckled. "And thank you for these beautiful tulips. Everyone will think I have a secret admirer."

Looking around and lowering his voice, Robert said, "You do. He's an honorable man, but his previous relationships have ended so poorly that he wouldn't think of inflicting himself on someone like Ms. Molly Ferguson. He's intimidated by her pedigree: daughter of a bishop, widow of a respected doctor and humanitarian. And her dedication: putting in so many unpaid hours for the church."

"Pedigree? Am I a poodle, then, or perhaps a Persian cat?" Grinning at his embarrassment, she continued, "Poor dear. I wonder who this honorable man is? What low self-esteem he must have! He could learn something from your graciousness, even to lowly receptionists." Smoothing a wisp of hair back into place, she said, "But I'm a bit old for admirers. Older than you, for instance."

Robert's face lit up with what others called his goofy smile. "Piffle. That couldn't be, and even if it were, what difference would it make?"

Before he could continue their repartee, the mahogany door to the bishop's office opened and The Right Reverend

Anthony Adams hurried out. Giving Molly a quick wave, Robert turned toward his Bishop, who boomed out, "Hey there, Bob!"

Robert winced.

"Heard you were coming over. Walk with me to the car; I'm chairing a task force for the mayor on revitalizing this town's civic spirit. Just up my alley. By the time I'm done, they'll be marching in the streets. What's this about digging up a box of ashes?"

"Yes, Bishop," Robert began, trying to keep pace. "We think they were buried in the garden a few years ago, along with some organist's shoes."

The Bishop was practically sprinting now. "Probably a prank by the youth of the parish, don't you think? You've got to keep those teenagers involved, Bob. Field trips to poor neighborhoods, gatherings with other churches, guitar music.

"Here's my advice," he continued. "Throw away the shoes and rebury the ashes. But be sure to put them in with the ones you'll be interring. That way, you won't have to eat the cost for the extra plot."

The Bishop stopped in mid-stride, nearly toppling Robert. "Now, Bob, about your demographics. They're all wrong. Too many underprivileged, too many middle-income seniors with no estates to leave to the church."

Robert had a retort ready about the youth of his parish not needing to travel far to see the underprivileged, but he willed his mouth to stay shut. Besides, the bishop wouldn't let him get a word in edgewise.

"Bob, heads up!" he was saying, "I want to see lots of kids this Sunday. I've planned a special children's sermon. Have them sit up front. And let's have music they can clap to. 'Kumbaya' is a good one, just the thing. And how many lifecycle events do you have scheduled for the service?"

To Robert's confused look, he boomed, "Baptisms, confirmations! You've got to keep up with the times, man. I'll loan you a few books."

"Thanks, Bishop *Tony*," Robert responded. Ignoring the scowl Bishop Anthony bestowed upon him, he added, "We have two baptisms and three confirmations. I'll warn you now, though, you're not going to like their demographics. One's a penniless student from The Sudan. Three are living at the Gospel Mission. You'll be happy to hear that one of the baptisms is a demographically perfect infant, the granddaughter of one of our middle income seniors."

They'd reached the Bishop's snappy blue sedan. Bishop Anthony answered, "Hrmph. That doesn't count. Her parents probably go to church in the suburbs, if they go at all."

Robert doggedly returned to his original subject, "Now Bishop, about the funding to repair our church tower. You may have heard that another piece of stone cladding fell off yesterday. Can you give me a list of potential donors and consider us for a loan from the capital fund?"

Bishop Anthony was edging toward the front door handle, but Robert stood in front of it. "The north entry is surrounded with hazard tape. Not very welcoming for your visit. If we had a loan guarantee, we could make some temporary—"

"Got to run," the Bishop interrupted. "There's not much return in fixing a church with no members." He pulled out his keys, unlocked the door with his remote control, and reached around Robert, saying, "You've got a vestryman with a plan to get a developer involved. Met him at Rotary. Good head on his shoulders." He reached the door and opened it onto Robert's backside. "Work with him," he called through the sedan's open window as it sped away.

Robert glared after the departing car. Hadn't the man noticed that Grace Church sat smack in the midst of hospitals, museums, and retirement homes? The nearest house with children living in it was at least five miles away. Hadn't he read the demographic studies saying the church at large was growing older right along with the population?

And that remark about working with Greg Chase and his developer friend ... He knew where that would lead. The church would be *developed* right off its property.

First things first. Where could he corral some kids? Maybe his friend Joe at what he referred to as *St. David's in the Suburbs* would loan him his Sunday school. Robert snapped his fingers. And he'd have the seniors bring their grandkids and coerce their parents into coming. Now if he could just convince Daniel to lead the congregation in a rousing chorus of "Kumbaya." With a last, wistful look at the door beyond which Molly sat, he walked toward his 1983 VW Rabbit, which he had to unlock the old fashioned way, with a key.

CR

To: RVickers@GraceSeattle.org;
Martin@GraceSeattle,org
From: DLaSalle@GraceSeattle.org
Subject: 1. Organ shoes: 2. Grace Church
Organists 1989-now: 3. KumbayUGH!

The Shoes:

Deacon Mary let me examine the shoes after I put on the plastic gloves. The label on the inside was faded, but I recognized the logo. It's a fleur de lis. Like this:

I recognized it because it's on the shoes my dad left me. His name is Peter LaSalle. I'm named after him. The shoes were made by the

Organmaster Company. I found them on the Internet. They're still in business after sixty years. These shoes were probably made in the early 1970s. The company representative told me that not too many of the patent leather ones were sold. And in those years, they only sold shoes on the East Coast. My dad got his in New York after he got paid for his first big concert.

Previous organists at Grace Church:
Charles Murray (2000 until I arrived)—

He came to Grace Church from First Presbyterian in Denver. He was competent but not dependable. He moved from church to church to play all the good organs. The choir didn't like him. He hardly let them sing. He had them hum along to the organ. He left for the Tracker organ at the Congregational Church in San Francisco. I think Ms. Lawrence's brother knew him.

Tim Evans (1990-2000)—

The older choir members told me they liked Tim. Even Henry the sexton liked Tim and he doesn't like many people. Mr. Evans was here ten years, and then left all of a sudden. No forwarding address. Everyone was upset. It wasn't like him. He didn't even send for his last paycheck. None of my organist contacts have heard of him. I haven't either. Maybe Ms. Lawrence's brother has.

Before 1990—

I couldn't find any records for the earlier organists. The pictures in the choir room go back a long ways, but no names. It looks like there was a lady organist during the 1980s and before that five or six men. Maybe some of the really old members of the church would remember. Or maybe there's a history of the church in the room labeled "Archives," the one that's always locked.

KumbayUGH!—

That's what we call "Kumbaya" at the Church Musicians' Conference. I WON'T play it on Sunday. Or ever. You can fire me. You probably don't know that there's no such word as Kumbaya, here or in Africa. It's a mangling of "Come by Here" and originated in the South as a spiritual. The title and the words in our hymnal are all wrong and don't do the original justice.

I have another suggestion. It's right in the hymnal, page 536. It's called the Torah song, and it's a Hasidic melody (that's Jewish). Each verse goes faster and faster. I'll teach it to the kids ahead of time and get them some tambourines to play. They can even dance to it. Around the Bishop.

Forward To: DDSLucy@funmail.com
From: Rvickers@GraceSeattle.org
Subject: 1. Organ shoes: 2. Grace Church Organists 1989-now: 3. KumbayUGH!

Lucy, here's some information from Daniel on former organists at the church, plus a few misc items I thought you'd enjoy. Would you mind talking to some of the old-timers to see what they remember? Also, when you contact your brother, could you ask him about Murray, Evans, and any others he might have known? As your reward, I'll have Daniel give you a tambourine to play on Sunday (Just kidding).

∾

Lucy's usually steady dentists' hands trembled a bit as she picked up the phone and dialed the number she still had memorized.

You have reached Thomas Lawrence, Master of Fine Arts, board member of the American Guild of Organists, representing organist Lisa Lawrence. If you are calling to schedule Lisa for a concert, be aware that she is booked through October. Other callers, please be brief.
Beeep.

"Thomas, this is Lucy. I'm afraid I won't be brief. First, I'm sorry we've been out of contact for so long. I dearly miss seeing my niece, and I have to confess I miss sparring with you on the state of the world and comparing notes on the Times' crosswords. And yes, there is a second reason I'm calling."

As succinctly as possible, Lucy recounted the discovery of the ashes and organ shoes, and asked if Thomas knew any of Grace Church's previous organists. She ended by inviting them both for dinner that weekend.

There! Now she could proceed to the next task in her new role as assistant investigator, a role she was eager to pursue. She'd done her best to keep busy since retirement by volunteering at the low-income dental clinic and chairing various committees at the church and Heritage House. But this project was an Inquiry into Truth that would draw upon the powers of intuition and perception she'd been nourishing with her daily prayer and meditation.

Stella and Luna were napping on the window seat. "Wake up, Lazykitties," she commanded. "It's time to plan for our meeting tonight." The cats raised their heads in unison, stared at her for a moment, and then nestled back into their cushions.

Chapter 4

"Let's review what we know so far." Deacon Mary's husband Joe stood with his hands on the back of their kitchen chair. Robert and Mary were seated at the trestle table, which was cluttered with papers, a box containing the ashes and organ shoes in their plastic bags, a plate of nachos and three bottles of beer. It was the evening of the first day, post discovery. "Robert, you start with what you know."

Robert tore at the beer label. "What I know is that I wish none of this had happened! Not the week of the Bishop's visit and with the tower about to fall down. My phone has been ringing off the hook with curiosity seekers. The vestry has called a special meeting to ponder the matter to death.

"And, Mary," he continued, "Your friend Lester and company from underneath the freeway have appointed themselves as tour guides. All day the garden has been full of people listening to their embellished version of the story. I imagine that for a buck or two they even turn over the turf where the box was uncovered."

He took a swig of beer and continued, "And of course all the people have attracted every pigeon in Seattle, and the Pigeon Lady, I mean Clare, is having a field day throwing pieces of bread all over. She promised the Health Officer she wouldn't feed them anymore, but I guess she's fallen off the wagon.

"Could you *please* get Lester and his friends to take a day off this Saturday? Maybe you can pay them something out of the discretionary fund to clean the place up. And ask Clare's guardian to take her to a ball game or something."

Mary was laughing so hard she couldn't answer.

"Let's get back to business," Joe suggested in the authoritative voice he'd cultivated in his Navy days. "I'll start. The label on the box of ashes says Massey Funeral Home, and the plastic ring serving as the seal has been broken. Now, Robert, did the police officer break the seal when she opened it, or was it already broken?"

"Lord, I can't remember. Mary, can you?"

"Of course not. Let's see, who would? How about Henry, our know-it-all sexton? Wasn't he standing next to the officer at that point?"

Robert shook his head. "Henry would say he remembered just to show off. We can't count on him. Let's go to the source. What's the officer's first name … Jane? Joan? Joyce! That's it. Let's see, Joyce Higgins? Joyce Holtz?"

"I know, I know!" Mary waved her arm in the air. "Hitchcock! Joyce Hitchcock. But how do we track her down?"

Joe sighed. "I'll do it. Be back in a minute."

Robert and Mary wolfed down nachos while they waited.

Robert sighed and said, "If the extravaganza this Sunday doesn't go well, the Bishop won't give us the money we need to stabilize the bell tower. He'll write us off as a lost cause. Then the city will come along and shut the church down as unsafe and the developers will move in. Were you able to rally the forces to get some kids for Sunday?"

"Mission accomplished." Mary saluted him smartly. "Lucy Lawrence was a big help. How organized she is! As we speak, she's meeting with the Heritage House residents who attend Grace to get some background on the earlier organists who might know something about these shoes."

Seeing Joe striding down the hall toward the kitchen, Robert and Mary pushed the nachos away and sat up straighter.

"I caught Joyce Hitchcock as she was going off shift," he told them. "She did break the seal, which means that the ashes originated in that box. But she doesn't remember seeing any name. The trouble is, Massey Funeral Home was bought out by Berman and Sons years ago. Assuming the box was buried after the lawn renovation two years back, that means that the ashes were someplace else for eight years or so. I'm going to have to check with Berman's to see if they inherited any unclaimed ashes from Massey's."

Seeing Joe rubbing his hands together in anticipation, Mary smiled fondly and said, "Oh, good, dear. Just the sort of project you love."

ষ্ট

Wednesday morning at 8 a.m., Robert stumbled out the front door of the rectory into the morning mist. That last beer at Mary and Joe's had been a mistake. Walking home in the rain had brought on chills and sniffles. And then Daniel had wanted to talk about his father. Mary was proving a bit too effective at opening the lad's floodgates.

Halfway to the church, he began sneezing in short sharp bursts and pulled out a tissue. As he wiped his face and glasses, he heard a murmuring sound coming from the sidewalk in front of the Memorial Garden. He looked up and saw some blurry birds. A lot of blurry birds.

He put his glasses back on and exclaimed, "Holy Christ!" Every pigeon in Seattle seemed to be standing at attention and facing the garden. Whatever they were looking at was hidden around the corner of the parish hall. It took him awhile to shuffle through the flock and see what looked like someone bedded down in the corner of the garden.

It was probably Lester again, but he'd better check. The pigeons parted obligingly to let him move forward.

He stopped five feet away from the figure. *Good God, it was Clare*, face swollen and purple on one side, the vein in her neck throbbing visibly. Robert rushed forward, taking off his coat at the same time. He put the coat under her head and wrapped her tunic closer. The birds' murmuring grew louder.

A large chunk of Wilkinson stone edged in crumbling mortar rested next to her head. *Oh, Lord, the tower must really be failing!* Robert squinted up just as a second stone broke free.

ନ୍ଦ

Lucy was enjoying a few extra moments in bed, remembering with a mixture of exasperation and satisfaction the outcome of the previous night's meeting. The members of Grace Church who lived at Heritage House had filled the largest table in the dining room. She wrinkled her nose, remembering the lingering steam-table aromas mingled with their colognes and aftershaves. She'd called the meeting to order after fifteen minutes of complaints, gossip and cooing over pictures of grandchildren.

"Father Vickers has asked us to help him solve the mystery of the crate that was dug up at Neola's burial service three days ago. You know, of course, that an unidentified box of ashes and a pair of organist's shoes were found inside."

"And they had red laces on 'em, don't forget that!"

It was old George who spoke—his tall, skinny figure tottering toward the table clad in shiny suit pants, unshined brogues, and a wrinkled white shirt. A few of the men gazed longingly at his shock of dazzling white hair. He'd been late as usual—not a good habit for the church's honorary crucifer, who was expected to head up every procession.

"Never seen anything like it," George continued, "and I've seen a lot in my ninety years. The only thing that comes close in the burial department is the time a seagull fertilized the top of Father Vickers' bald head as he was leaning over to bless the remains. Never laughed so hard in my life. Almost dropped the cross."

That's nothing new, Lucy thought. She decided to intervene before he could launch into another story culled from his sixty years' membership at Grace Church.

"I'm glad you're here, George. You can help us gather information about the organists who served before Daniel, so we can ask them about the shoes. We should also try to remember anyone who left the church suddenly, for no good reason, in the past ten years."

"How about that brother of yours?" George cackled. "He left all of a sudden. Isn't he an organist?"

"That's true, George," she sighed, "and I have contacted him."

Three of the attendees were looking at their watches and whispering, prompting her to query, "Is there anything you'd like to share with the rest of us?"

Midge Taylor spoke up. "Um, Lucy, we need to leave for a few minutes. We're expecting a phone call."

"You're all expecting a phone call at the same time?"

"Well, within a few minutes of each other."

"Oh?" Lucy recalled being in Midge's apartment a few weeks earlier when Deacon Mary had called. Midge's voice had quavered uncharacteristically as the two of them said the Lord's Prayer together over the phone. She'd been under the weather recently, Midge told Lucy; that was why the deacon was calling.

Lucy glared at the three of them. "You don't mean to tell me that you've conned our overworked, kind-hearted deacon into calling you all every night! I strongly suggest that you say you've recovered, thank you, and that her calls will no longer be necessary." The ladies nodded meekly and crept off.

George piped up again. "It's a darn shame that Neola and Fred have gone to their rewards. One or the other would have gotten to the bottom of this, especially since it happened at Neola's own funeral. That gal knew everyone—being head of the church women's guild—and Fred was the Senior Warden. Knew where all the bodies were buried. Get it? All the bodies—"

"Yes, we all get it, George," Lucy answered. "Now let's go around the table, one at a time. Does anyone remember Tim, the organist who was here in the 90s? I understand he was a youngish man in his forties. He stayed for ten years and then left suddenly. You first, Elsie."

"Oh, dear, I'm sure I don't know," murmured Elsie, ducking her newly permed head.

"Come on, girl," George shouted. You were lead soprano in the choir, and a darned good one! If anybody knows anything, it's you."

"Well," Elsie blushed, "that Tim was a nice boy. I recollect that he came recommended by our retiring organist; that would be Mrs. O'Leary. She'd heard him play on a trip to visit her relatives in Des Moines, Iowa. He was a single man, but so friendly and cheerful that he never lacked an invitation to dinner or a place to spend the holidays."

She continued, "And Henry—he was the groundskeeper then, before he was named sexton—he followed Tim around like a puppy. We never could understand why, Henry having a tin ear and all, but Tim treated him real nice. Many's the time I'd arrive early for choir practice and see the two of them at the organ console, Tim playing the keys for the chimes, and the horn, and all the low notes, just for Henry's enjoyment."

"By gum, you're right, Elsie!" George burst in, white cowlick shaking, ruining Lucy's round-the-table agenda. "When Tim up and disappeared, Henry acted like his brother had died, all weepy and mopey. I told him to snap out of it and act like a man. Hooey! He didn't much like that, but at least I riled him up enough to get a little of his spirit back. Now, Lucy, I'm of the opinion that Henry should be spoken to about this matter. I'll gladly volunteer."

"And I'll gladly consider it, but don't do anything yet," Lucy answered, thinking, *Please, dear God!* "Now, can we move on to the next person in the circle without further interruption?"

The others hadn't been able to contribute much. One long-time member remembered that Tim liked to chew spearmint gum. Another theorized that the ashes belonged to a former rector who'd run off with the church secretary in 1960. When the conversation devolved into an argument over what was for dinner the next night, Lucy adjourned the meeting.

Lucy was returned to the present by the cats, mewling as if at death's door because of a fifteen-minute breakfast delay. She'd fed them and had a fresh cup of coffee in hand when the ringing phone interrupted her reveries again. The display read Thomas Lawrence. Was she ready to speak to her brother?

"Aunt Lucy. It's Lisa, your long-lost niece. You haven't called me for ages. I've missed you so much and I've got so much to tell you. Dad's out of town and I just got back from a concert in Denver, and I'm graduating from high school in June—"

"Lisa, Lisa, stop for minute!" Lucy exclaimed. "Let me catch my breath. Dear, I'm so pleased to hear from you."

The two caught up over the next fifteen minutes, and both apologized for being out of contact for so long. Then Lisa asked about the ashes, the shoes, and the organist, proclaiming it to be the coolest mystery ever.

Lucy asked, "Lisa dear, do you remember the red laces I gave you for your organ shoes when you were eleven? Do you still have them?"

"No, Aunt Lucy, I haven't seen them for ages. Guess what? I wear pink laces now for breast cancer awareness, in honor of Mom. Dad tried to stop me, but I told him I'd refuse to play without them. It's gotten me some great publicity."

Lucy congratulated her and then asked if she'd seen the red laces in the past two years. Lisa assured her that she had not.

"Can we really come over for dinner this weekend? Don't worry about Daddy. I know he's been missing you, too. I'll pump him beforehand about that organist and do some Google searches. And, Aunt Lucy? Do the cooks at Heritage House still make that heavenly cherry cheesecake?"

☙

Robert sprawled on the grass, arms wrapped around Clare, foot throbbing. The falling projectile had been closer than a man with no depth vision could register. He'd only had time to throw himself over Clare, who was stirring now. A number of people had descended upon them. Henry the sexton was in the lead.

"I told you that tower needed to come down! Look at this mess! Rocks all over, pigeons, and that dol-gurned bird lady!"

"We're injured, but conscious, thank you, Henry," said Robert. "Now would you stop your bellyaching and call an ambulance for Clare? Call the police, too."

"What do we need with the police? The stones fell off that old tower like I told you they would."

"Do it, Henry!"

Daniel ran up. "Father Robert, you're alive!" Robert found himself enveloped in a bear hug, Daniel's voice shouting in his ear. "I saw it. I saw it."

Henry stared at the organist, and then demanded, "Saw what?"

"The rock falling from the tower, heading straight for Father and Bird Lady Clare! The pigeons were crying, so I looked out the window of my room. That's when I saw it."

"Did you see anything else?" Robert asked in a low voice.

Tilting his head back, Daniel stared at the top of the tower and then lowered his gaze slowly to the ground. His brown curls shook a slow "no," paused, nodded a slower "yes," reverted more slowly to "no," back to "yes," and then stopped in the middle. "I'm not sure," he murmured miserably.

Robert had struggled to a sitting position. "Never mind now. We'll talk later. Here, give me a hand."

The Medic One team had arrived and was hurrying toward Robert and Clare. Henry bumped into them as he ran from the office, shouting, "See, I was right not calling the cops." He pointed toward the street. "The lady officer who was here the other day just drove up, right behind the medics."

"Guess I'll have to set up a substation here, Father, with all the calls we're getting," drawled Officer Joyce Hitchcock as she approached.

Robert looked up. "Officer Joyce—I mean Officer Hitchcock. How did you hear about this? We hadn't called the police yet."

"Oh, whenever I work the graveyard shift I listen to the scanner after I get home to help me get to sleep. That's how I heard the call for Medic One about this lady getting bopped by a rock in your graveyard garden. I live just south of here, so I decided to see for myself."

Robert noticed a red pajama top peeking out above her bullet-proof vest. "I'm glad you're here." He gestured her to come nearer, then crooked a finger at Daniel. "Officer, I think someone dropped those stones through the tower window."

"But Father Robert," Daniel protested, "how could you

tell? Your glasses were off, and anyway you told me you don't have any depth vision."

Robert grimaced and said, "Why don't you tell her about my bunions, too? Of course everything was a blur, but when I was moving to help Clare, I looked up and saw some movement in the tower opening. I couldn't say who or what it was, but I'd bet my *MAD* magazine collection that stone didn't just fall. That's why I asked if you saw anything out of your window, Daniel."

Daniel shuffled his feet. "Father ... and Officer Joyce. This is going to seem strange, I know, because other people have told me it's strange, but it's just the way my mind works. I know that you want me to get off the dime, but you'll have to wait. I just need to go into the church and play the organ for about fifteen minutes. It calms me down, and then I can recreate a flash-frozen picture in my mind of the whole scene. All the way from the top of the tower to the feathers on the pigeons."

Glancing at Robert apologetically, he continued, "Eidetic memory, that's what I have. It means that I have total recall. Plus the doctor told me my peripheral vision is extraordinary. Off the charts, he said. People don't realize that peripheral vision goes up and down as well as side to side. I've also got 20-10 vision. In both eyes.

"If the organ weren't there, I could use the piano, or listen to the radio, but the organ works best. So if you'll excuse me, I'll just go play. When I have the picture clear in my mind, I'll report back." Daniel backed away slowly, then turned and ran toward the church.

"What should we do while we're waiting for him to solve the mystery?" Officer Hitchcock asked Robert. As if to answer, Henry lurched toward them—pushing, pulling and shoving Lester and his buddy Pete.

"Arrest these men, officer! They're the ones that caused those rocks to fall!"

Chapter 5

A half hour after Henry's accusation, Mary arrived at the church, carrying a box of donuts. Lester had refused to say a word until his "counselor" arrived. Mary wasn't surprised that he'd asked for her. Lord knows she'd served him in nearly every other capacity—meal ticket, confidante, shoulder to cry on, and negotiator with various city officials. She'd even dog-sat for Spike—Lester and Pete's communally-owned German Shepherd—when the two decided to ride the rails to Portland one weekend.

The Memorial Garden was surrounded by even more hazard tape, and a red flag planted by Officer Hitchcock marked the spot where Clare and Robert had fallen. Mary noted with interest that the marker pierced the same patch of lawn where the box of ashes and organ shoes had been uncovered.

Lester and his fellow detainee Pete sat on the ground, guarded by the shovel-carrying sexton. Father Robert and Officer Hitchcock sat chatting on one of the garden's stone benches. Luckily it wasn't raining today. The final notes of something by Bach hung in the air.

"Mother Mary!" Lester had spotted her. "Tell this lame excuse for a janitor to wise up. He thinks we tried to kill the Bird Lady and Father Vickers. Just because we—"

"Shut up, man!" cautioned bandana-clad Pete. "They

can use anything you say to incriminate you."

"Calm down, guys," said the officer, ambling toward them. "Lester, you've got your counselor here, so why don't we start at the beginning. First of all, Mr., ah, can I call you Henry? Where were you when all this happened?"

"Me!" barked the sexton. "I've got nothing to do with this!"

"Be that as it may, just answer my question."

It turned out that according to Henry, he'd come in early to give the building an additional spit and polish before the Bishop's visit. He'd been dusting the books in the library when he heard Robert's cry.

"Lester and his criminal buddy must have been in that tower, because—"

"Enough said," Officer Hitchcock answered. "We'll let them tell their own story. Lester, I assume you're the spokesman."

Lester swallowed the last of a donut and then finger-combed his thatch of wiry, gray-brown hair before facing the group. He spoke loudly over Henry's spluttering. "Ladies and gentlemen, our actions in this matter have been entirely innocent. Firstly, I will make a full disclosure here and tell you that I and my friend have in actual fact visited the top of this church tower. But not today we haven't."

The spectators stared at him, obviously not satisfied.

Lester hurried on. "Secondly, allow me to summarize our defense for trespassing on Father Robert's property in one brief phrasing, taken from a cowboy hymn I learned as a child." Lester looked heavenward before proclaiming, *"Heaven is so high, and I'm so far down."* He slapped his baseball cap against his thigh for emphasis and paused again, expectantly.

Deacon Mary said, "That's a nice image, Lester, and I have no doubt that you'll be using it to illustrate the rest of your eloquent speech. As your Counselor, I have a piece of advice. Finish what you have to say, make it quick, and no truth stretching."

"Yes, Mother," Lester said. "Now if you'll just allow me to continue for another minute. See, this bottom rung of the totem pole we're so far down on—with all due respect to my Native American brother, Pete, and many other street citizens too numerous to mention here—this totem pole stands in for many things we indigent members of society endure, but I'll just mention two ... or three.

"We, the homeless, have nowhere to conduct our daily activities except the sidewalks and parks of this city. We obtain our daily bread by advertising our situation to motorists when they stop for a red light. A few kind hearts hand us *down* a buck or two. The rest just look *down* their noses. And here's the best example that I was saving for last. At night, we have nowhere to lay our weary bodies down, get it, *down*, but underneath the noisy freeway, with its toxic fumes and all. Are you catching my drift here? Not to mention being pelted with whatever people feel like throwing *down* over the guardrails."

"Tell it, brother!" yelled Pete.

As Lester told it, the guys looked for every opportunity they could to rise above the rest of humanity, if only briefly. When Lester and Pete had discovered the exterior door to the church tower unlocked one day, they climbed up to check out the view. Back on the ground, they figured out a way to prop the door open so they could repeat the heady experience. No one had noticed, since overgrown bushes hid the tower door.

The last few times they'd come, the door had been fastened with a simple padlock "that any amateur could get through." The last time they'd climbed up was last night, to view a rare late winter sunset. Lester had refastened the padlock, "So help me God."

At this point, Henry interjected, "I found this shirt caught in the tower doorway." He held up a faded flannel shirt. "It's *his!*" He pointed at Lester.

"As for the door being unlocked, " Henry said, "I fastened that padlock myself the other day, after the funeral. Now the chain has been cut and the door is open, and you're looking at the ones who did it. I don't know how that door got unlocked in the first place, but you can't expect me to carry the weight of this whole place on my shoulders!"

Lester, on the defensive, shot back, "You sniveling liar! Like I said, anyone with a lick of sense can get by a padlock without having to cut the chain. You don't see me carrying any bolt-cutters, do you?"

There was silence all around.

Lester spat on the ground and said, "My case rests."

The silence was interrupted by Daniel, who'd arrived after completing his Bach piece. "But it wasn't Lester or his friend in the tower this morning. It couldn't have been."

"Why not?" Henry had found his voice. "You've seen Lester in this flannel shirt a million times, and furthermore, it's still warm and it smells like him and those nasty cigarette butts he keeps in the pocket. You'll notice all he's wearing is a T-shirt, even though it's forty degrees out!"

"You know why it was there, you old coot!" Lester yelled.

Before Officer Hitchcock could intervene, Daniel walked in between the two and stood next to Lester. "But I've remembered now. I knew that playing the organ would help. The person I saw in the tower was wearing a green mackintosh."

"A what?" the group chorused.

"A mackintosh. It keeps the rain off your clothes."

"Where do you come from, man?" Lester said. "Out here they call them parkas or windcatchers, or maybe it's windbreakers. Nine folks out of ten in this area wear them, except us homeless, who have to make do with garbage bags or nothing."

Daniel nodded uncertainly and continued, "But the person had his back to the tower window, so I can't give him a name, not yet. Except that it was a "him," and he had dark brown hair. It wasn't long and it wasn't short. It was darker than yours, Mr. Lester. And Mr. Pete, your hair is even darker and longer, so it wasn't you, either. I've seen the person who was in the tower before; I know I have. And Father Robert, I know it wasn't you, even though you have some dark hairs. You were down here protecting Miss Clare. Don't worry, Mr. Lester; I'll remember eventually."

"Thanks buddy, but it may be too late," said Lester, as Officer Hitchcock came toward him with her handcuffs at the ready.

"Sorry," she said," but I need to take you and Pete in so the detectives can interview you. Daniel, don't leave the church. The detectives will want to talk to you later. Henry, give me that shirt so I can bag it for evidence. Now, gentlemen, I don't think I need to use these cuffs or demonstrate my martial arts skills, do I?"

"No, Ma'am," they mumbled, staring up at her imposing figure. As he and Pete passed Mary on their way to the cruiser, Lester said to the deacon, "If we're arrested, post our bail at Godfather Bail Bonds. Gino owes me a favor," he added in a whisper.

Mary nodded. "Anything else? What about your dog?"

"My friend Harry's got him today. But you might want to check on Clare's flowers. They could use some weeding." He looked her in the eye. "Mother Mary, I don't like her, but I sure don't want her dead."

Mary sighed and nodded. She knew that what Lester said was true. And leave it to Lester to remember that Clare had adopted the unkempt planter boxes the city had installed on the sidewalk below the church. She'd appropriated plants from a nearby park, fertilized them with pigeon manure, and watered them by dragging the church hose down the street.

As Lester and Pete settled in the back seat of the cruiser, Mary sighed again, waved, and murmured, "God Bless."

❧

Fifteen minutes later Robert stood alone in the middle of the Memorial Garden. His foot throbbed exquisitely. Mary had gone to the hospital to be with Clare. He'd refused the aid crew's offer to take him in as well, but was regretting the decision already. Henry was patrolling the perimeter of the church, and Daniel was with his nine o'clock organ student.

"Here I am," Robert mused, "the senior rector of Grace Parish, the 'Mother Church' of the city, surveying my domain on one foot."

It had started to rain, plastering the remaining hairs to his head. The fastener on his clerical collar had sprung and the white ring hung askew. One of the lens on his glasses had also sprung and now rested in his muddy hand.

Looking toward the street, he recognized a blurry but familiar figure approaching, the last person on earth he wanted to meet in his condition.

The visitor drew near and exclaimed, "Why, Robert, you're a sight for sore eyes. Perhaps we could adjourn to the inside of the church so you can dry off. And since you're standing on one foot and grimacing, let's put the other foot up. I'll fix us a pot of tea and relay to you a message from the Bishop. I'm very uncomfortable with this, but he's designated me as his emissary. He said he would have come himself, but was late for the Seamen's Ministry meeting down at the waterfront."

"Hello, Molly," Robert sighed. "I wish we were meeting under better circumstances. You look lovely in that bright red raincoat. I'm awfully sorry, but I'm going to have to put my muddy hand on your shoulder while we make our way inside."

Settled in the office with a towel around his neck and foot raised, Robert gave Molly a lopsided smile and asked how her superior knew about the latest stones falling from the tower.

"Three people called to report it," she replied. "The first was a garbled message about God avenging the unholy. The second caller didn't give a name, just said that someone had been hurt by a falling stone and the church needed to be closed down as a safety hazard. The third caller was someone named Henry. I see from your rolling eyes that he's known to you. He said to tell Bishop Adams that the rocks in the tower are so loose that a bum who lives nearby was able to pry one loose and throw it down into the garden, not once, but twice, ruining at least one rhododendron."

"I don't suppose," Robert commented, "he mentioned that one of the stones hit a woman named Clare on the head, causing serious injury, and that the other one landed on my foot. As soon as I get this foot fixed up, I'll brief him. I suspect that the stone was deliberately pushed. I wonder who the first two callers were."

"Oh dear, how awful!" Molly exclaimed. "Well, I'd better follow the Bishop's orders and relay his official message. Bishop Adams said to tell you, quote, that this is just about the last straw for Grace Church, end quote. He wants a full report and action plan waiting for him on Sunday."

She looked at his disaster area of an office. "If you want, I could help you create a clean spot on your desk before you begin. Lord knows the thunder and lightning that will follow his learning that the injury was serious. I suppose it would be too much to expect that he'd be worried about your foot. But *I* am concerned, and now intend to escort you to my car and take you to the emergency room."

Robert didn't protest, and fifteen minutes later, after he'd hobbled to the rectory to change his clothes, they were on their way. As she negotiated traffic, Molly told him that his wasn't the only church in hot water with the Bishop. Another congregation, which would remain nameless, was in the midst of a juicy scandal involving the assistant priest, the church treasurer, and a trip to the Bahamas.

Then Molly said, "I'm seriously thinking about switching churches, Robert. St. Brendon's was my husband's family's church, and, frankly, I find the liturgy and music boring. Maybe I should consider Grace Parish. I hear that your new musician can play the socks off the organ, and that you give some powerful sermons." Her comment was greeted with silence.

After thirty seconds or so, Robert croaked, "Molly, don't. Please, don't."

"Don't do what?" she asked, glancing over. "Robert, what's wrong! Are you going to faint?" She pulled over to the curb.

His face was pale, forehead sweating. "Lie back, Robert," she murmured, taking a limp hand. "Breathe in. Now breathe out." His pulse was erratic, but strong. Molly waited, and after a moment, Robert's cheeks turned pink, very pink, as if he were blushing.

"Thank you," he said, looking out the window. "I'm much better. And now you've seen my hysterical side. After I have this foot looked after and get some rest, I'd like to explain. I don't always react so strongly when someone wants to join our church."

"I certainly look forward to hearing what you have to say. I'm not used to being turned away at the parish gate," Molly replied gravely.

As Molly resumed driving, Robert, eyes closed, felt the scalp prickles that often signified the voice of God ordering a course correction. He'd dreaded the moment when he might be romantically interested in a church member. He'd taken the position at Grace Church to escape just such a situation.

It had been seven years ago, just about the time that far

too many clergy of all denominations were facing charges of sexual harassment by women who felt that their ministers had taken advantage of their pastoral relationships. Some turned out to be cases of unrequited love on the part of the parishioners, some involved consensual relationships that had gone bad, and some were clear cut cases of seduction and abandonment on the part of the clergy. As a result, many of the women had been directly or indirectly forced out of the churches they'd grown up in and loved.

In Robert's case, the feelings between him and his parishioner Susan had been mutual and tender. She'd joined his previous church two years into his residency. As a young woman, she'd been a Roman Catholic nun and was in her early forties when they met.

Her unworldly and shy nature had appealed to his overdeveloped sense of compassion and protectiveness. The congregation knew about their relationship and approved. But when he proposed marriage, Susan declined, saying she'd come to realize that her vocation was as a single woman devoting herself to environmental causes.

This had been Robert's first serious relationship since his first and only wife had decided fifteen years earlier that she couldn't be a clergy spouse and physician at the same time. Sandy had been like a rambunctious horse: the perfect companion when well-fed and rested, but when she was on a mission, watch out. He still missed her vitality. And now, for a second time, someone he loved had left, not for another person, but for a different sort of life. It was as if they'd both used him as a springboard to launch themselves into new adventures.

Well, his spring was sprung—not that Molly would use him for that purpose. She was a mature woman with nothing to prove.

The parish couldn't understand why Susan and he had parted, but the rumors had placed the blame on him. Susan had done her best to quell them, even offering to leave the parish, but after a lot of soul-searching and a talk with his then bishop, he'd begun looking for another position.

Now here he was falling in love with the bishop's secretary. Darn it, where else but at church was a spiritually inclined person to meet another spiritually inclined person? Certainly not at the *MAD magazine* convention, which he attended discreetly each year. And he was loath to consider Internet dating. Picture it: *Myopic, balding priest seeking religiously inclined female for marriage. Must be willing to attend services, preferably every week, but at least once per month, and help out at the coffee hour afterwards.*

But maybe, just maybe, he'd succeed in wooing and winning this wonderful woman Molly without falling into the traps he'd been unable, perhaps unwilling, to avoid until now. Was it possible he could enlist Molly's help in doing so? By God, when the bishop's visit was over and done with, he'd give it his best shot.

Chapter 6

Joe Martin arrived at the church at 11:30. He and Mary had a lunch date, but Joe was prepared to wait. There was no way his wife could be on time and accomplish the errands of mercy she'd described over the phone. After visiting with Clare at the hospital, she was driving 'cross town to the police precinct to try to spring Lester and Pete.

Joe absently rubbed his hands together as he surveyed the police-tape snaking around the Memorial Garden. He followed it through the small jungle of rhodies and around the corner of the building to the tower door. The area, invisible to both the garden and the street, had obviously provided habitat for various urban animals, insects and humans. The ground was littered with the usual droppings and discards. As he expected, there was a separate piece of tape stretched across the padlocked door. He wiped a spider web off his jacket as he threaded his way back to the garden.

Emerging from the bushes, he spotted a lone pigeon on the lawn. The bird had breached the tape and positioned itself next to one of the stakes. Joe bet it marked the spot where Clare had fallen. A stray sunbeam lit the tableau.

Daniel approached and stood beside him. They watched in silence until another rain cloud shadowed the area. The organist spoke. "Hello, Mr. Martin, sir. It's Daniel, remember? I play the organ here. Do you happen to know where Father Robert is? Not that I'm not wanting to see you also, it's not that. I was just thinking I could tell him a few more things I remembered about when the stone fell. Oh. Maybe you don't know."

"Hello, Daniel," Joe said, turning to face the younger man. "Of course I remember you. And Mary called and told me everything. She also told me about your phenomenal memory for details." A beatific smile lit up Daniel's face, and Joe smiled in return.

Behind the organist, Joe noticed a man striding toward them from the curb. Thank God plainclothes detectives had stopped pretending they were in the cast of *Miami Vice*. The unbuttoned shirt and gold medallion around the neck had given way to the old standby: a too-small sportcoat worn over baggy Dockers, silver handcuffs dangling from the pocket.

"Well, Daniel," Joe remarked, "it looks like you'll be able to talk directly to the detective."

"Do you think you could stay with me, sir? You know, to translate?" Daniel asked, nodding his head in encouragement.

"Translate? But you speak English just … Oh, I think I know what you mean. I'd be honored."

"Is one of you the fellow claiming he has a photographic memory?" The detective glanced at a notebook in his hand. "Daniel L-a-s-a-l-l-e. Is that pronounced La-sally?"

"With all deep respect, officer, no, it isn't," Daniel answered. "It would be if there were two ee's on the end, but there's only one, so it's the French pronunciation, which is Sal, as if you were going to say salad. No, that's not quite right; it would be more like solid. Or somewhere between the two."

Joe intervened, "Daniel here asked me to run interference." Joe introduced himself to the relieved detective, adding his professional credentials.

As the three men walked around the garden, pointing and talking, Henry rounded the corner of the rectory and detoured over to add his two cents. The noise level around the group increased considerably, supplemented by the clatter of wings as Henry swiped at the pigeon with his spade.

The bird barely cleared Mary and Lucy Lawrence, who had just arrived from opposite directions. Lucy spoke first. "Mary, I just heard about the accidents. Is Father Robert all right? And the lady who feeds the pigeons?" Without waiting for an answer, Lucy continued, "Do you think there's a connection with what happened at the internment? Why, it looks as though the stone fell right on top of the burial place!"

Mary, with patience born of long practice, waited.

Lucy caught herself and asked, "Oh, Mary dear, how are you? Is that your husband I see? You weren't involved, I hope?"

"No, Lucy," Mary answered, "we're supposed to be meeting for lunch, but Joe appears to be otherwise occupied. Would you like to join me? We'll compare notes."

Lucy protested that she was wearing her sweatsuit and walking shoes, and Mary laughed, assuring her there'd be no problem. Calling to Joe to meet them at *Dim Sum City* when he was done, Mary escorted Lucy to her Mini-Cooper, watching sympathetically as Lucy carefully folded herself in.

By the time Joe joined them at the restaurant, both women had a tidy stack of empty plates in front of them. "What did you find out?" they chorused, but he held up his hand.

"Not until I eat."

"Watch this," Mary told Lucy. Joe and the server bowed to each other and chatted a minute in Mandarin. The server pointed at the plates on the bottom shelf of the cart and smacked her lips. He took a sample of each.

"Eew, chicken feet," Mary cried.

"Good guess," replied Joe, his mouth full. "The claws are the best part." He crunched down. "Delicious. A great source of calcium."

Lucy changed the subject. "I don't mean to be flippant, but this situation at the church reminds me of when my cats get into the knitting basket. The different yarns get all wound up until they're impossible to separate."

Wiping her mouth, she continued, "Within the space of three days we've unearthed organ shoes with red laces, along with human remains, and had stones falling or being pushed off the church tower, all in one little garden plot. Do you think Clare and Father Robert were intentional targets? Is it a coincidence that all this is happening while the church is under the bishop's microscope?"

"Why Lucy, that sounds just like the blurbs on detective novels," Mary laughed. "But, speaking of Clare, do you realize that she always feeds the pigeons at the very spot where we found the box of ashes and where the stone fell? When I got to the hospital, she was conscious, thanks be to God, and communing with her feathered friends lined up on the windowsill."

To her companions' incredulous look, she said, "It's true! Don't you remember the story about the Tribal elder who was in the hospital down at the State Capital? The eagles flew outside her window until she died. Anyway, Clare seemed to recognize me, but as usual didn't say anything. She did let me hold her hand."

Mary speared a dumpling from her husband's plate. "It was the first time I'd seen Clare without her hood. She's quite a beautiful woman. Her caretaker Ann was there and told me that Clare was once an East Coast socialite who had a breakdown in her thirties. Ann wasn't sure how Clare had come to be here or how she'd developed her love of pigeons. A trust fund pays her to make sure that Clare has housing and other necessities."

"Poor Ann told me," Mary paused to chew, "that she felt responsible for what had happened, because she'd stopped for a latte on her morning walk with Clare. While she was negotiating with the barista over non-fat versus skinny, Clare snuck off to the churchyard to visit her feathered friends."

After Joe was served a few more delicacies from the cart, Mary reported on her visit to Lester and Pete. They'd still been waiting to be questioned at the precinct station.

"That cheeky man asked me to call the Mayor's Office for him," she said. Apparently Lester had been appointed to the Homeless Task Force as a "client representative" and wanted to let them know he couldn't make the meeting.

"By the way, where's Robert?" she added. "I hope he got his foot looked after."

As he sipped tea behind a tower of empty plates, Joe held up a finger. Pushing the plates carefully to one side, he answered, "According to Henry, Robert went off with some woman in a fancy red car. He said the word "woman" like he meant "hussy." I don't understand why that man's so intent on biting the hand that feeds him. Robert should have fired him years ago for general orneriness.

"Anyway," he continued, "Daniel told us the other thing he saw with his X-ray eyes. There were no more facing stones missing from the tower, meaning that both stones must have been deliberately dropped ... or thrown, since they ended up in the garden instead of the doorway."

The detective and Joe, trailed by Henry, had made their own inspection. The group then climbed up the inside of the tower. Of course Henry had resisted their entry, but pulled out the padlock key after one look from the detective. Daniel, afraid of heights, stayed on the ground.

There were four loose facing stones lying on the tower floor. At first Henry claimed to know nothing about them, but soon admitted that they'd been there for years—on the chance that repairs were needed. As to whether any were missing, he maintained that his job kept him too busy to keep inventory on every loose object in and around the church. But *if* they'd been thrown, Henry repeated, it was by Lester, not some brown-haired guy in rain gear. Daniel was seeing things.

"You can say that again," Mary exclaimed.

Lucy said she also had something to report, as well as someone for them to meet, but thought perhaps they should wait until Father Robert returned from his joyride with the mysterious woman. They agreed to reconvene after that evening's Eucharist service.

છ

A cloud bank over Puget Sound hid the March sunset, and a cloud of sweet incense hovered over Mary, Joe, Lucy, and Father Robert as they sat in the dimly lit church. The prodigal priest had returned just in time for the five o'clock service and was met by old George, who'd been at the incense again. He'd decided to practice for the upcoming Bishop's visit, swinging the censor in figure eight patterns. He'd done it perfectly as a younger man, but his skills were now rusty at best.

Robert couldn't bear to tell old George right now that this bishop hated incense, and that it wouldn't be allowed on Sunday. For this small evening service, it fit the mood, so long as George could avoid hitting anyone with the brass container.

The thump of Robert's foot cast added a satisfactory counterpoint to the cadences of the prayers and readings, and the ten persons attending the service left feeling satisfied and spiritually fed.

Now Robert was resting his leg sideways on the faded rose velveteen seat of a darkly veined fir pew at the front of the sanctuary. Jesus, Mary, and various saints loomed above in the muted blues, greens, and violets of the stained glass. The cream-colored Holy Spirit hovered over them all.

Joe, Mary, and Lucy had stayed after the service and were eating from a bag of potato chips Mary had smuggled into the church. Father Robert was venting. "Won't I cut a fine figure next Sunday, galumphing around in this thing? A crippled priest in charge of a broken-down building could be the last straw the Bishop warned me about via Molly, ah Ms. Ferguson."

Robert had told them about the message that the Bishop's secretary had relayed that morning and had stoically endured their teasing about being chauffeured to the doctor in her fancy red car.

"We know now that it wasn't loose facing stones from the tower that caused the injuries … at least, I'm pretty sure we do." Robert continued. "Granted, the tower does need shoring up, but it shouldn't be an excuse for closing down the only historic church in our diocese. Another bishop would use the occasion of his visit to launch a fundraising drive."

He straightened up in the pew. "And if he won't, maybe I will. I'll invite the newspapers and announce the fund drive after the Bishop's sermon." He paused to reposition his foot and continued, "And then maybe we'll hold an auction, where the auctioneer yells out big dollar amounts and everyone competes to be the most generous. What do you think?"

Mary and Joe were toasting him with chips when they heard the side door of the sanctuary open and close. A man appeared and then stopped to survey the surroundings. A casual bystander would label him prosperous, well fed, and desirous of making an entrance.

"Thomas! Over here," Lucy called. That very afternoon her estranged brother had returned her phone call and agreed to come to the church. He made his way to the end of the front pew where she was standing, took both of her hands, and kissed her on the cheek.

Ignoring the audience in the pews, he said, "Lucy, you are the most exasperating woman I know, and the most stubborn." He paused. "But how I could let my own bullheadedness keep you from your niece, I'll never know."

He turned to the others. "Hello, Father Robert, and Deacon Mary; it's good to see you both again after a year's absence." Looking at Joe, he added, "You must be Mary's husband. Forgive me for dragging you all into my act of contrition, but I know that you're Lucy's friends and therefore know about our estrangement."

Lucy started to speak, but Thomas had more to say.

"Lucy was my bossy big sister, and I got mighty tired over the years hearing that I was too big for my britches, had tunnel vision when it came to my career as a musician, and was turning my daughter into a clone of myself."

He turned back to Lucy, bowed his head slightly, and said, "You were right. Thank God Lisa inherited your spunk and started talking back to me. If you hadn't called, she would soon have insisted I take the initiative. We're pleased to accept your dinner invitation. You're the only immediate family we have, and we're yours. Nothing, not even your or my egos, is strong enough to break that bond."

A collective sigh rose from the audience.

In response, a smiling Lucy said, "Hey, Tommy, do you know why the organ was invented?"

With a big "Ha!" Thomas stood on his toes and answered in a voice an octave higher than his own, "No, sis, why was the organ invented?"

"So the organist would have a place to put his beer!"

Thomas' sputter sounded just like someone exhaling beer through his nose.

The audience waited.

Lucy continued, "And did you hear the one where the patient says to the dentist, 'It must be tough spending all day with your hands in someone's mouth.' And the dentist says,

'No, I just think of it as having my hands in their wallet.' "

The audience laughed heartily, along with her brother.

"That's a good one, sis," Thomas said. "In all these years you haven't lost your touch with a joke."

Beaming, she addressed the audience. "That's how we used to make up when we were children. I'd tell him the latest joke and then he'd laugh and play me a piece he'd learned recently. In the interest of time, maybe you should play later, after telling us what you know about Grace Church's previous organists. Despite the tragic incident today, I think it's important to identify whose remains we found on Tuesday."

Thomas nodded. He tipped his old-fashioned fedora and removed it, revealing a balding head and shoe-polish-brown hair, in contrast to Lucy's graying, light brown pageboy. Beneath the dark green raincoat, which he removed and draped over a pew, he was wearing a dark suit and white shirt.

The side door opened again and slammed shut. The reverberating echo seemed to propel Daniel into the sanctuary. Seeing the group in the pews, he screeched to a halt. "I'm sorry," he said in a stage whisper. "I thought the service was over. Oh. This must be a contemporary service. No music. The priest in the pews with the people. And potato chips instead of communion wafers?"

"The service is over, Daniel," Robert answered, "and some of us are snacking. Say, Daniel, would you mind joining us for a minute? I'd like you to meet Ms. Lawrence's brother."

Daniel's eyes opened wide. "Thomas Lawrence, the organist? Yes, yes, I do want to meet him."

Thomas turned to greet him, and Daniel exclaimed, "Oh, my. You certainly look like the man in the tower. But you're not. You're balder. And I don't think you'd wear a Macintosh over your suit. Oh, but is that your green Macintosh on the pew? Anyway, I'm honored to meet you, Mr. Lawrence. I've played a number of your compositions. On the organ."

Thomas Lawrence started to place the fedora back on his head, but then seemed to remember he was in church, and tugged at the bottom of his suit jacket instead. Then he shook Daniel's hand. "Ah, the new young organist. I've heard about your way with words. It doesn't matter, though. Not if you can play."

"Oh, I can, sir, I can." Daniel answered.

"I'll put you through your paces later. Now, Lucy, Father, what's all this about a man in the tower?"

The others provided an abbreviated account of the morning's events. Lucy had already told Thomas about finding the ashes and organ shoes and their need for information on Tim Evans, the former organist.

After assuring them he was otherwise occupied when the stones were falling, Thomas said, "Tim Evans. He was one of the reasons I decided to attend Grace Church when I moved to Seattle twelve years ago. I wanted my daughter Lisa to be exposed to the best organ playing this third-rate city had to offer. I could never understand why he didn't play for the Roman Catholics. They have the best instruments and acoustics."

To the line of raised eyebrows along the pew, he continued, "I can tell you what happened to Tim. A good friend of his died; I think the man was a former lover. Tim holed up in his rooms for a few days and then decided to go to Minneapolis where his friend was being buried."

Thomas continued, "He didn't tell me this himself; I heard it from an organist friend living in Minnesota. Apparently Tim knew he'd be in no condition to play for months, so he packed up his things and left. No one's heard from him since, and I doubt he knows anything about your strange discovery."

He paused. "Curious, though, that he disappeared not long before your mystery person appears to have been buried. We could take a wild flight of fancy and say the ashes are

Tim's. Or, who knows, maybe Tim came back with his friend's ashes and seized the opportunity to bury them when the garden was dug up."

Joe, who had been closely following Thomas' account, asked for the name and number of the Minnesota contact. He watched with envy as Thomas located it with a few clicks on his smart phone.

Thomas turned to Daniel. "I also knew your father, Peter LaSalle."

The younger man fixed his deep brown eyes on Thomas's face.

"He set a high standard. We trained together at the Eastman School and kept up our friendship even after he divorced your mother. Sad business, that. It broke his heart to leave you. Quite unnecessary, but he was a man of principles, even if the principles were wrong-headed. He actually thought you'd be better off without him. Strange, though, I haven't heard from your father in more than ten years. I do hope he's still alive."

Daniel sprang up, tears appearing to fly from his eyes. "He's not dead! I know he's not. Here, I'll show you." He pulled a wallet out of his back pocket and removed an envelope folded twice over. "My father wrote me last October, telling me about the organist position here."

Father Robert reached for the letter, but Daniel pulled his hand back. Robert sighed, and said, "I always wondered how you knew about the job before it was advertised. It seemed too good to be true, having someone appear on our doorstep, ready to roll. Your dad must have heard about it through the grapevine that every profession seems to have. But how did he locate you?"

Daniel was silent, but his fingers roamed along the back of pew.

"It's obvious that he's been keeping track of his son," Thomas said. Daniel nodded long and hard.

Mary's husband Joe stopped his fidgeting and thrust out his hand. "Can I see the letter, please?"

Daniel promptly handed it to his new friend.

The others peered over Joe's shoulder as he studied the letter and envelope, which was postmarked Chicago. "It was written on a word processor," Joe said, "so there's only the signature to identify the handwriting. And only three letters—D-A-D. Mr. Lawrence, does this look like Peter LaSalle's writing?"

Thomas answered, "I may have one of his letters in my files. I'll check."

"Daniel, do you recognize his signature?" Joe asked. But Daniel was running toward the exit, with Mary in pursuit. She called back over her shoulder, "Very sensitive, Joe."

"I wish I knew how to investigate and be sensitive at the same time," said Joe. "Mary's the master, although she'd never admit it. I'll bet she comes back with Daniel's life story and a good guess as to whether his dad is still alive."

After agreeing to compare notes the next evening, the group disbanded. B-day, the bishop's visit, was only two and one half days away, Robert reminded them. "We've got to get to the bottom of this by Sunday, or Grace Church will be on the endangered species list."

CR

"Hey Joe," Robert asked as the group was leaving, "while you're waiting for Mary to calm Daniel down, can we talk for a minute?"

"Sure. We've probably got an hour if we need it," Joe answered, coming to sit next to Robert in his pew.

While Robert stared toward the marble altar for a good three minutes without speaking, Joe waited, as he'd done with many others during his career. In the meantime, he mentally reviewed the plans for a hutch he was building.

Joe's main concern about moving from their home to a condo had been giving up his workshop, but Mary had found a place in their price range with not only that, but also a pool, rooftop deck, gym and concierge service. And just around the corner on the side street was a place where he could indulge in his other hobby, beer brewing. He'd resolved to spend more time on his hobbies and less time hovering over Mary.

"Joe, you've lived through your fifties," Robert began. "Why is it that no one who's gone ahead tells you about all the storms that come up? I know about the midlife crisis stuff. The church tends to call it "the dark night of the soul," for God's sake, but that's not what it's like at all.

"You're lucky, Robert" Joe answered. "At least those catchphrases give you a little warning. In the business world, you suffer in silence and don't have a clue what's going on."

Robert threw his leg, cast and all, up over the pew top. "So you understand what I'm getting at. Don't you agree that they've got it all wrong, this crap about running away with your secretary or quitting work to become a helicopter pilot?" He shook his head. "I don't want to run anywhere, but this past week—hell, this past year—I've haven't accomplished squat."

"Yep," said Joe, and then shut up. It wouldn't help Robert if he launched into his own version of what he called "the midlife slam."

Robert rambled on, "Up until now, I've glided right through life without too much trouble. Sure, I've missed not having a wife, and being a priest is a pretty lonely calling. It's not a good idea to get too friendly with parishioners and my professional colleagues would rather compete to see who can sacrifice the most for their parish rather than go out for a beer. But I've done pretty well on my own, and up until now, I've figured out a way to handle most of what comes my way."

He continued. "Sorry Joe, I'm trying to make a point here, but I'm not sure what it is. The point is ..." He paused, and then turned to look at Joe. "The point is, I can't do it on my own any more. I don't have the stamina. I don't know how to deal with crumbling buildings. And …"

Joe stared at the altar while Robert choked out, "I feel so guilty, so responsible for what happened to Clare! I should have shut this place down the minute the first tiny piece of stone came off that tower."

"You know Robert," Joe said, "If it makes you feel any better, I don't think there's one of us who hasn't experienced something like this. Not being able to handle a situation. Losing confidence. The guilt. And you're right, no one talks about it. There is something that seems to happen as we get older. I think you're right on about the stamina thing. It's harder to pick ourselves up."

Now Robert waited while Joe thought so hard he felt his circuits crossing. "And if we've got the right stuff in us, we give up." Joe paused, looking perplexed. "Robert, I have to tell you, I don't understand what I just said."

Robert thought, and then spoke. "I think that's it. You give up. You 'Let go and let God,' as they say in A.A. You ask for help."

Joe let out a deep breath and smiled, "Well, since you've asked, I can put together a list of suspects and then enlist Officer Hitchcock's help us find out who threw that stone."

The side door to the church slammed and Mary trudged in. "I think Daniel's calm enough to go to bed, and that's where I want to be in just a few minutes."

"Okay, dear," Joe answered, "I just need to schedule a brief follow up with Robert."

Mary swayed a little. "Go ahead and finish. I'll just nap in this pew." She sat down, and then disappeared from view.

What sounded like a clap of thunder rattled the windows. The lights dimmed and then brightened, but not to full strength. Robert looked up and located a burnt out spot on the high walls that flanked the altar. He chuckled and then laughed outright. "Look, Joe," he said. "Up there where the angels holding trumpets are carved into the plaster. One on each side of the altar. I think they call it 'bas relief.' Although I'm probably pronouncing it wrong. Anyway, look! The light illuminating the angel on the left is out. So now we have one dark angel and one light one."

Joe laughed, too. "You know I'm not the most spiritual person around, but I have to say that being watched over by the angels of dark and light just about sums up my belief system."

Joe went on, "Okay, here's my assessment of the situation. I'm inclined to believe that this is a case of a stone thrower for hire. Daniel's eyewitness account eliminates most of us as suspects, and given the average age around here, the rest wouldn't have the wherewithal. Lester's a possibility—his hair is more brown than gray—but if he was the one, there's no way he'd stick around afterward."

"Maybe it was one of the others who hang out under the freeway," Robert said.

Joe paused while another clap of thunder rattled around.

"Are we sure that was thunder and not another attempt to topple the church?" Robert said, half rising from his seat. Just then a flash of light beamed through the stained glass representation of the resurrected Christ over the high altar, followed a few seconds later by an unmistakable thunderclap.

Joe pointed up. "Look Robert, a miracle! The dark angel is lit up again!"

"A very good omen," Robert answered. "But back to the subject at hand … if someone was hired to throw the stone, who put this person up to it? And why?

"You know who I think?" Joe answered. "Henry. That man's got an attitude problem a mile wide. I think he's getting old and tired and wants out. Anyone else would just retire, but he's got too much pride."

Robert took his taped-together glasses off and rubbed his eyes. "So you're saying he figured that if he caused enough mayhem, the church would close and he'd be off the hook? But I can't believe he'd want Clare or anyone else hurt."

Before Joe could answer, Mary's voice interjected as if emanating from a disembodied spirit. "Of course he wouldn't, and I don't think he has anything to do with it. Don't ask me why. I can't tell you; it's just a feeling."

With that, the session came to an end.

CR

It hadn't worked, trying to shut down the church. He'd called the city anonymously to give them a report, but they could care less. It was an historic building, they said, so unless the stones were falling on the street, they'd forward the matter to the preservation commission. He didn't have that long to wait.

Then he'd called the head office for all the Episcopal Churches in the area. A woman saying she was the Bishop's secretary answered. *Bishop!* They must be in cahoots with those Catholics from Rome. "The bishop knows all about it," she told him, like it was no big deal, and then she said that he'd be visiting the church this Sunday.

His duty was clear. He'd go to that poor excuse for a house of God and talk to the guy man to man.

"What would Jesus do?" That's how he'd put it. "Jesus would say his disciples are more important than buildings," he'd tell him. "The Lord would say all I need is one rock for my church, not a whole pile of them, that the greedy should get behind me, Satan." If that didn't work, he'd just have to use his secret weapon.

CR

First thing Friday morning, Rick Chase was leaning over a conference table covered with architectural drawings. His short, stocky colleague Cliff faced him from the other side of the table, wearing a leather coat over his Nordstrom's striped shirt and tan cords. A matching leather cap lay at the table's edge. Rick didn't have any meetings, so was dressed in jeans and a black T-shirt under a plaid flannel shirt. Both men wore variations of the cowboy boot.

"Your guy does great work, Cliff," said Rick. "So, let's see. Here's the overlay of the condo on top of the rectory and the food bank. And the parish hall is renamed as an 'event space'—not much change needed there. You know, the church calls it the Great Hall for some reason; that might be a good name to keep. It sounds British. Then the Memorial Garden; that'll have to be spruced up—maybe paved over so there'll be enough space for outdoor parties and receptions."

"We won't have to remove the ashes or remains or whatever you call them, will we?" asked Cliff.

"I don't see why," said Rick. "Another English touch. You know they bury their Kings and saints under the floor of their cathedrals. All we'll need to do is put a little plaque somewhere. It would be tacky to put the names right on the pavement.

"Hey, this is great," Rick continued, "You have the fence surrounding the whole property. We'll keep it locked when there's no event and have a secure entry from the condo."

Cliff looked at the spreadsheet next to the drawings. "This thing has to pencil out. The condo will have retail space at ground level—florist, dry cleaners, a bakery. But you know how hard it is to fill those spaces." He looked up at Rick. "What about all the scruffy folks who hang around that area?"

Rick didn't hesitate. "They'll leave when they can't get handouts from the church and food bank. This area is gentrifying, and I'm working with the zoning folks to get the hygiene center on Ninth Avenue closed."

"Hygiene center? What the hell is that?" Cliff jabbed the spreadsheet with a pencil.

Rick smiled. "Got you on that one. A place with showers and a Laundromat. For people who live in their cars or on the street. Could be us one day, eh, buddy?"

Cliff walked over to the window and looked down. "Yeah, right! I'd jump off this building before I'd sleep in a car." He walked back, "Let's get a move on."

"Oh," Rick said, "You heard about that street person being hit by a stone from the church's tower yesterday. That really bolsters our case for re-development of the property. I called the Bishop's office today and reminded them of their potential liability, especially now that two people have been injured. I decided not to leave my name. Too bad about Father Vickers getting his ankle smashed."

Cliff barely nodded.

Rick jabbed his own pencil at the drawings. "Okay, let's review the schematics. We, I mean, the church, call this building 'the sanctuary.' There's another good word, as in, 'The art museum's annual fundraiser will be held in The Sanctuary.' Once those heavy pews are gone, its possibilities as a multi-use space will be endless. Anything from a medieval banquet to a symphony concert. And weddings … there'll be lots of those. You know, most of Grace Church's income comes from people wanting to be married in a beautiful old church, just like Stacy and I were."

He paused. "And it is wicked beautiful. I wonder if there's a way we could keep the pews, put them on rollers or something." He smiled.

Cliff drummed his fingers on the table. "What about the Bishop saying the deal is off if they can't hold one service each Sunday and two on Christmas and Easter. That's going to impact our schedule big time. And those—what do you call them—*altars*, need to go."

"No they don't." answered Rick. "The lower altar can be

moved out of the way, and the one against the wall, believe me, you don't want to get rid of that. It's Carrera marble, made for a big Catholic Church in New York that couldn't afford it. One of our city fathers went back there and had it shipped out. That altar and all the tile mosaic, not to mention the stained glass, will draw the historical and arts folks. We can take the cross off and store it. The only concessions we'll need to make to the Bishop are to keep the cross on top of the building, maybe even enlarge it, and the sign out front that says 'Historic Grace Church.' We need to keep all the things I'm mentioning to maintain the building's landmark status."

Cliff picked up his cap and snatched up the spreadsheet. "That better be it, or the whole deal is off."

¡

After waking at 6 a.m. on Friday morning, Robert paced back and forth across his attic hideaway, planning the fundraising campaign to save the church tower. That would be his "action plan" to present to the Bishop. He smiled. Maybe they could stage an old-time revival featuring the Church of England equivalent of a fire-and brimstone preacher. Instead of an altar call, they'd have a clothespin call, using the method of the early twentieth-century evangelist Aimee Semple McPherson: clotheslines strung over the pews with clothespins attached; the audience exhorted to pin paper money to the line, which was then moved toward the altar via a pulley arrangement.

Instead of a thermometer showing the progress toward their goal, they'd have a one-quarter scale replica of the tower rise in the middle of the Memorial Garden. Each donor would place a stone on top of the pile.

Robert stopped pacing and stared out the dormer window. Fantasizing might lift his spirits, but it wouldn't get the tower rebuilt. He'd never had to raise a serious amount of money and didn't have the temperament for the job. They'd have to hire a professional, who'd want to mount a campaign to hector everyone who'd darkened the door of the church for the past sixty years.

Then they'd want to hold an auction. He detested those. At the last one he'd been dragged to, people in tuxedos and strapless dresses had cavorted around tables groaning with food, waving paddles. One barely missed smacking him in the forehead. They called it paddle-raising. *I'll give one hundred dollars. I'll give one thousand. I'll give my first born.* Mass hysteria. Totally unspiritual.

Then, to further depress him, there was Daniel's situation. The poor boy was holed up in his room, considering the possibility that the letter from his long-absent father was a hoax. He certainly couldn't be counted on to raise the rafters on Sunday.

℞

At eight a.m. Joe put down the phone and rubbed his neck. He was almost certain he knew whose ashes had been unearthed on Tuesday and was feeling the letdown that frequently followed a discovery. Just as in his working days, he had found it satisfying to be absorbed in solving a complex puzzle, one that covered the metaphorical whole table, leaving no space for the routine grind.

Instead of enjoying proper meals with loved ones, you'd munch pizza from a napkin, staring at the puzzle. You couldn't spread out the newspaper or touch your wife's hand as she put down a mug of coffee, but it didn't matter, not while there were pieces that still didn't fit. Then, just before you began tearing your hair out, it all fell into place. You were on top of the world and, with a flourish, you swept the pieces back into the box.

But until the tabletop re-accumulated enough keys and

papers and coffee stains, it was possible to sit there and see your reflection and wonder at the look of defeat in your eyes.

The letdown he felt was familiar, but the sadness wasn't. He should have kept his meddling fingers out of it. The problem was, he'd been bored since retiring a year ago. Following Mary on her deacon's rounds, trying to keep her out of trouble, wasn't stimulating enough for a former insurance investigator who loved puzzles. And he could only spend so much time on his hobbies. Worse, Mary was beginning to resent being shadowed, and that just wasn't acceptable. They had too many good years ahead of them. In the meantime, he might as well organize his notes.

He'd decided to track down Tim Evans, the church's former organist, who'd left suddenly ten years earlier. Using the information supplied by Thomas Lawrence, Lucy's brother, he'd called Minnesota and reached a gentleman named Georges ("That's Georges with an s," he had been told), who was eager to reminisce. Joe soon learned all there was to know about every organist active in Minnesota during the past twenty years. One of them had been a man named Nathaniel Bellamy.

"Nathaniel and I," Georges explained, "were of an era when one's sexuality was not discussed, especially not in Minnesota. Our title was 'bachelor' and we were much in demand as escorts, dinner guests, and confidants. Nathanial, to his credit, served as a mentor to many younger musicians, gay and straight, including Tim Evans. The two of them became lovers, but lived apart."

After a fifteen-second pause—intended, Joe realized, to pique his interest to a frenzy—he obliged, "And then?"

Georges answered instantly, "After a year or so, the young man apparently tired of the subterfuge. Gay Pride had reared its ugly head in Minnesota. Tim became involved with the community—quite a number of the community, if you get my drift—and broke things off with Nathaniel."

According to Georges, the older man took the breakup philosophically but turned into somewhat of a recluse. He was, however, kind enough to recommend Tim for the organist's position at Grace Church in Seattle.

"Soon afterwards, he died of a heart attack, poor man."

Joe asked, "If Tim had left the relationship, why was he so broken up when Nathaniel died? At least that's what Thomas Lawrence said."

A lengthy pause followed a long intake of breath. "Regret, my dear, pure and simple. For what might have been. Tim paid a pretty price for his callowness and promiscuity. And, I suppose, Tim had loved the old boy in his way. He came back for the funeral and stayed on after. *Oh, my*, the music at that funeral!"

Joe interrupted to ask what had happened to Tim, and learned, without too much delay, that his health had declined rapidly afterwards. By that time there was an AIDS hospice in Minneapolis. That was where Tim spent his last days. There had been no funeral that Georges knew about. ("And I would have known.")

Georges admitted ignorance of the fate of Tim's remains, but speculated nonetheless. "There's a group of younger gay men who seem to have all the time in the world, ah, God bless them, to care for people like Tim. Possibly one of them assumed the role of executor."

"Does the name Peter LaSalle ring a bell?" Joe asked.

"Vaguely. He might have been one of the volunteers at the hospice. I wish I had the constitution to empty bedpans and such, but *quel dommage*, I don't. Of course I donate and go to the fundraisers. They're quite amusing, actually."

After a few prompts, Georges found the phone number for the hospice, and Joe rang off with all due haste. His next call was mercifully shorter and to the point.

The Hospice director, a Mr. Lauderback, checked his records and confirmed that Peter LaSalle had been on their roster, and that volunteers often helped the patients with burial arrangements, since so many of the dying were estranged from their families.

"He may well have helped Mr. Evans in that way," the director continued, "although, unfortunately, we'd have no record of that. Our records do indicate the date Mr. Evans died, however. His body was taken by Remlinger's Funeral Home here in Minneapolis. I see on our exit summary that there was no local funeral."

Mr. Lauderback was obviously a careful record keeper, and within a minute Joe learned that Peter LaSalle had resigned as a volunteer soon after Tim's death, for unspecified personal reasons.

"We like to make sure our volunteers are cared for also," the director added, "but apparently Mr. LaSalle dropped out of sight or I'd have a record of his forwarding address and so on. Now it seems that you want to know what happened to the remains. I'll give you Remlinger's number; they keep very good records. Or would you like me to call them? You would? My, I feel like a real detective!"

Joe, never one to turn down an offer of help, encouraged him effusively and wished the man a productive data search. He'd be surprised if the remains hadn't been sent to Seattle for burial at Grace Church. And he'd be even more surprised if Henry the sexton didn't know all about the arrangements, including the red-laced shoes.

He'd better let Robert know what he'd learned so far.

CB

Daniel opened the refrigerator door and stared inside. Every morning Father Robert turned the milk and bread and fruit and butter and orange juice and some other things into a breakfast for the two of them. Making tea in the microwave was the only thing Daniel could do. His one attempt to toast bread had set off the rectory fire alarm. But Father Robert hadn't come down from his room yet, and it was seven o'clock.

Daniel had been awake most of the night wondering if his dad was alive, but it hadn't affected his appetite. His skinny frame demanded regular feeding no matter what the circumstances.

A hungry person had to take chances, so he grasped the carton of orange juice with both hands, carried it gingerly to the counter, managed to extract the plastic safety ring after a try or two and poured a big glassful, spilling only a little. Then he pulled two slices of bread out of the package on the counter and spooned a big chunk of hard butter on each. He rolled the bread around the butter and was just lifting the confection to his mouth when the phone burst into song—that tune where the lyrics are about finding yourself in trouble and how Mother Mary comes to you and lets it be, or something like that.

As much as Daniel appreciated the opportunity to save money by living at the rectory, he was tempted to move every time the phone began bleating out the music that Father had chosen as a ring tone. What was worse, Daniel couldn't answer right away to put the song out of its misery. He had to wait for the whole refrain so Father had the first chance to pick it up.

The song stopped suddenly, and Daniel took a quick bite, glad that Father Robert was at least awake. He was chewing contentedly when a loud cry ricocheted off the walls and down the stairs. The bread and butter lodged in Daniel's throat and his strangled coughing mingled with the cry.

"Daniel, Clare has died! Dear God! How could you take her?" The anguished appeal accompanied Robert's footsteps down the stairs from the attic.

CR

Once again the side chapel of the church was occupied with Father Robert, Daniel, Deacon Mary, Henry, Officer Joyce Hitchcock, Lester, and Clare's caretaker Ann. No one had been inclined to turn on the overhead lights. A candle flickered in the lamp hanging over the altar.

Joe slipped in without being noticed. He'd come to tell Robert what he'd learned about the mysterious ashes and to browbeat Henry into confessing what he knew, but at the sight of the somber group, he revised his plans. He stood in the shadows, listening.

"Remember the other day when she was feeding her pigeons in the middle of all the excitement over finding the ashes," Officer Joyce said. "It was like I'd time-traveled back to the Holy Land and was standing in front of the temple." She noticed the surprised looks on the faces of her companions. "You shouldn't jump to conclusions. I served my time in Sunday School."

Lester snuffled loudly into his shirt sleeve, then turned to Ann. "You were always trying to drag sister Clare back home when she joined us by the freeway entrance while we panhandled. That gal sure did make a splendid figure in her robes. Our take was always bigger on those days."

Ann was snuffling, too. "All of you were such good friends to her. Next to the birds, you were her closest companions."

"Not me, I wasn't," groaned Henry. "I could have saved her when she was lying there yesterday. Instead I was the Bad Samaritan, hurrying on by. Just couldn't wait to get to my mop and broom. I'm a wicked man and don't deserve to work here."

"Henry," Robert responded, "I have to say I've questioned your priorities in the past, but your words just now show you are a true Christian. We need you at Grace Church now more than ever, and if you're truly sorry, this is the place to do penance."

"I have a confession, too," said Daniel. "I let Miss Clare come into the church to listen to the organ. Not that she couldn't have come in on her own. During a service. But she couldn't have brought a pigeon with her. So during the week, I let her bring one in. And one other time I let her bring in two. That time we had to run around and clap so they'd come down from the rafters. We checked for any messes before we left. Both times. And the one time there was a mess, we cleaned it up so well you'd never know it had happened. Oh. If I hadn't just told you."

"Oh Daniel, you're an angel," Mary whispered.

Joe came over, sat down, and gave his tearful wife a hug. After a moment he asked Officer Joyce, "Is this a murder case, now?"

"Assuming someone pitched that stone to the ground and it didn't just fall, it's manslaughter at the very least. And if they were aiming at Clare, it's murder," she added.

"And there's the assault on Pastor … I mean, Father Robert. The problem, as usual, will be to prove it, assuming we can track down Daniel's man in the tower."

"I thank the good Lord that man wasn't me," Lester declared, "and moreover, I thank Him that I was able to assist the police in their investigation, once they discontinued their obsessiveness with pinning the crime on this homeless bum."

He stood up, faced the altar, and continued, "Lord, You were guiding me, your servant, yesterday morning, when me and my buddy decided to wash up with the hose next to the tower door. You guided my hand when I took off my shirt so as not to get it wet and then you moved me to place that shirt over the handle of the tower door, thereby discovering that the door was in fact ajar and the chain cut and the door propped open by a crowbar. A crowbar, Lord that I'd never seen before in that location. And, Lord, if I hadn't heard the thump of the stone as it hit the ground and Father Robert's scream, I could have pulled that crowbar away from that door, thereby trapping the criminal in his lair. But one man can only do so much Lord, and I know—"

Robert interrupted, "Lester, this is a time to remember Clare, not a revival meeting."

Deacon Mary looked up, "Meeting? Oh my gosh, the research person from the University's sociology department was supposed to meet with Clare tomorrow morning to observe her feeding the pigeons. I don't know how to contact her to cancel."

"Say what?" asked everyone simultaneously.

Hands clenched into fists, she answered, "Haven't you heard?" Mary's pixie face turned hard. "It's the latest fad, following bird lovers around. It's not enough for the social scientists to put criminals and poor people and racial minorities under a microscope; now they're harassing people like Clare.

"Oh, but I'll figure out a way to find the woman to give her the news," she continued; "I always do. Everybody's mother, that's me. But you know," she said, her throaty treble uncharacteristically loud and belligerent, "Clare treated me like a sister. An equal. She was Mary to my Martha, the one who met the world head-on and dragged me with her. I would have never met Lester, Pete and the others if it weren't for her."

None of the rest said, "There, there" or tried to jolly her out of her anger. This was what wakes were for.

Fifteen minutes later, after a closing prayer, the group descended the stairs leading to the garden and gasped at the shimmering mound of flowers, balloons, and teddy bears that rose before them, along with many, many bags of bread crumbs and bird seed. Pigeons flew about, lighting one by one on the heap to coo and chirp.

A group of twenty or so humans stood at the base, paying their respects. Robert recognized two of Clare's fellow pigeon caretakers and some residents of the surrounding apartments. He was surprised to see Mr. Perkins, who had monitored Clare's activities from his window with binoculars and complained regularly that her feeding program would surely result in an avian flu epidemic.

A spot of bright red approached the group from the right. Robert squinted. It was Molly! Before he had a chance to greet her, a second woman approached him, hand extended. She was wearing a bronze suede jacket over boot cut jeans with bronze suede boots. The breeze was lifting her bronze pageboy into horizontal wings.

"Father Vickers, hello, I'm Kate O'Reilly with KORN 8 News. I'd like to give you and Clare's friends and family an opportunity to share your thoughts with our viewers in an exclusive interview. Our deadline is in five minutes, so if you'll all move over here in front of the memorial, we'll begin." Without waiting for an answer, she turned and shouldered her way through the crowd, shouting, "Move over. Press."

Robert knew he'd have to make a statement but wanted to talk to Molly first. She was probably here with another message from the Bishop, and he'd better find out what the official spin was before submitting to Ms. O'Reilly's interrogation.

He turned to the others. "Ann, Mary, ah, Lester, do you want to be interviewed?" Ann and Mary said "No" in unison and walked over to greet the mourners. Lester puffed out his chest, hesitated, and then followed the women. Daniel, Joe and the sexton were nowhere to be seen.

"I'll be back in a minute, Ms. O'Reilly," he called, heading toward Molly. The reporter barely nodded; she was busy instructing the camera operator to get close-ups of the pigeons.

"Robert, you should run and put on a clerical collar over your T-shirt and jeans before representing the church to the public," Molly chided as he approached.

"And you should stop wearing red if you want to maintain our professional relationship," he responded. "Molly, what does His Eminence want me to do about this? Play it up? Play it down? One thing I won't do is remove the memorial. In fact, what I'd like to do is play it up, as the beginning of our efforts to restore the tower in Clare's memory."

"Then you should," she answered, "because you've got nothing to lose. The Bishop says to tell you he's washed his hands of the whole thing. Grace Church will sink or swim on its own, with no help from the Diocese. He's going to say as much in his sermon on Sunday."

Robert spluttered in response, "Maybe he can control the Diocesan purse strings, but not the pockets of its people, or these people, or the people of this city! Thanks, Molly. See you on the evening news." He saluted smartly before turning toward Ms. O'Reilly, who was on the ground with her mic, trying to coax a sound bite out of one of the pigeons.

"Wait, Robert," Molly called. She came to his side and put some bills into the pocket of his T-shirt. Here's your first donation."

Chapter 7

"Eat up, Daniel. This may be one of our last meals before we're kicked out of the rectory."

Daniel's head rose from its position directly over his Saturday morning pancakes. "We have to leave? Why? What did we do? It wasn't that high water bill from last month, was it? When I was composing the prelude in the shower? You can take it out of my wages."

Robert speared a piece of bacon. "No, son. I'm going to tender my resignation at the special vestry meeting later. It's the least I can do after spouting off on TV yesterday. There's a picture of me in the paper this morning surrounded by Clare's mourners, half of whom live under the freeway, backgrounded by the pile of flowers and birdseed left in her memory, and, of course, the pigeons. The headline says, "Priest Tries to Save His Flock." Maybe it would be best if Grace Church disposed of its assets, such as they are, and relocated to the suburbs without me."

Daniel stirred a piece of pancake around a puddle of syrup. "Oh, Father, I hope that doesn't happen. I know how hard it is to find a job. I'd been looking for months before I got the mystery letter about the organist position here. If it was my dad who wrote it, I'd like to stay here in case he wants to visit. Even if he came incognito, just to hear me play."

He continued stirring, and said, "But that's selfish of

me. I only board here, and can leave a forwarding address. This is your home and you've fixed it up just the way you want it. You preach good sermons and help people. And you have lots of friends here." Daniel glanced quickly at Robert and continued, "and now you have a new friend, Miss Molly."

Robert looked at him with affection. "You're not selfish. I'd love to see you reunited with your father. The vestry won't kick us out, at least not right away. I'll let you know what happens at the meeting."

Daniel stood up. "Do you mind if I practice now and wash the dishes later? I have an idea for a piece to play at Miss Clare's memorial service, and it would be better if I composed it away from the shower, so the bill doesn't get too high."

At ten fifteen, Robert exited the rectory. He planned to arrive a few minutes late to the meeting so the vestry could give free rein to their sentiments. The more steam they let out beforehand, the less there might be to blow off at him. As he approached the church, he wondered what surprise waited in the courtyard today. Lester and company, including the communal dog, Spike, were serving as a rag-tag security crew, guarding the growing pile of flowers and other items left by Clare's mourners. Nothing these guys did would surprise him.

Uh oh, he thought. Loud voices, barks, and pigeon squawks. He stuck his head around the corner. Lester's security team was in heated discussion with two pant-suited women wearing long rubber aprons and carrying nasty looking clippers. As he watched, the women began circling the floral monument, plucking out prime specimens.

"Look here!" exhorted the shorter of the two. "This is church property, and we're representatives of the church. Our Bishop is visiting tomorrow and we require a few of the roses from this pile, maybe a dozen. And a bunch or two of carnations and whatever else is fresh. These flowers will be wilted by tomorrow anyway without any water." She turned to her companion. "Ginna, go over and cut the last of the rhodies off that bush. Make the stems good and long. They'll fill the vase at the entrance."

Robert decided to intervene before Lester became a loose cannon. Stepping around the corner, he called out in his best rector's voice, "Why, Mrs. Peters, the altar guild is certainly getting an early start. No wonder, with the big service tomorrow. You'll have lots of extra work creating special floral arrangements, polishing the silver and all that. I certainly do appreciate your efforts."

Mrs. Peters' lips turned up slightly. Lester's turned down.

"I'll bet your flower order was larger than usual this week," Robert continued. "It's a good thing there's so much money in your guild account. Why, I'll bet you could fill all the vases with orchids if you wanted," he chuckled, adding quickly, "Just a little joke. I know how thrifty you are. Wonderful shepherds of the church's resources."

Mrs. Peters plucked a final flower, and then rose to her full five feet two inches. "Father Robert, some of us have time to chat, but we guild ladies have work to do. Ginna, come away." They hurried into the church, trailing rhododendron leaves.

Lester took off his baseball cap and slapped it against his knee. "I'm sure glad you came along when you did, Father. That lady is a dead ringer for the one who beats me in my nightmares with a frying pan when I've had a few too many."

"Carry on, men. And dog," Robert saluted as he headed toward the church entry.

He emerged an hour later, wiping his forehead with his shirt sleeve. Eviction averted, for now. The vestry had actually appreciated the publicity garnered by his TV appearance. Already this morning ten calls had come in asking for the time of tomorrow's service.

They'd spent the rest of the hour poring over the registry of Sunday services, marriages, baptisms, and funerals for the past year. Bishop Adams was a stickler for detail, and would want a strict accounting of everything. The vestry debated whether to note the participants in the annual animal blessing as "congregants," and decided against it.

To further brighten Robert's morning, Molly had called. After they flirted back and forth, she resumed her role as diocesan secretary and relayed the bishop's requirements for the next day. He wanted a hot cup of coffee, two sugars, to be waiting for him. And real cream—none of that powdered stuff. After reviewing the service records and inspecting the entire facility, he'd need assistance donning his vestments for the service.

"He'll be bringing his own robes," she explained, "and his big hat and that staff with the hook on the end—the items whose names I'm afraid I've forgotten. And he expects that your robes won't clash with his."

Robert snorted, "That's going to be impossible, because I'm wearing the multi-colored number the Sunday school presented me with, the one that's covered with outlines of the kids' hands. The hat is called a mitre, by the way, and have you noticed that the shorter the Bishop, the taller the mitre?" He paused, and receiving no answering chuckle, decided to try again. "His shepherd's staff is called a crosier and I'm afraid he might use it to bring me into line."

This earned him a sigh, a cluck, and additional instructions. "When the opening hymn begins, the procession is to proceed in this order: the crucifer carrying the largest cross you have, Deacon Mary carrying the biggest Gospel Book you own, at least four altar servers of the same height, the full choir, and someone behind the Bishop to keep his robe straight."

"Why, there will be more people in the procession than in the congregation," Robert noted. "And does he want me to be the one who carries his train?"

Molly parried, "Dear me, he didn't mention you at all."

Robert huffed, "Good. I'll stand outside down the hill and order the ambulances on their way to the hospital to turn off their sirens before they pass the church. You know how His Nibs can't stand distractions."

"One last thing," Molly murmured. "Remember now, I'm only the messenger. The Bishop watched the six o'clock news last night, and he wants all the flowers and mementoes left for Clare—which he describes as 'that pile of daisies, bread crumbs, and birdseed,'—gone by tomorrow morning."

After ending the call, Robert, in accordance with his new resolve to ask for help, decided to gather together Mary, Joe, Lucy and Lester to advise him what to do about the Bishop's edict. But first he had another errand to run. After tracking down his prey with a phone call, he called a cab to take him down the hill. He couldn't walk decently with the leg boot.

Framed vertically by tall buildings on either side, Elliott Bay's waters gleamed at the end of the street. Before Robert's eyes a huge orange shape emerged from the building on the right and moved to the left, blotting out the seascape. It took a minute to realize that it was a container ship heading south to the port.

His clerical collar reassured the Saturday security guard at one of those tall buildings that he was the caller who needed to see the distraught parishioner on the twenty fourth floor. It helped that the guard turned out to be a lapsed Roman Catholic who retained his respect for "the Fathers."

The elevator whooshed him up and opened with a discreet *ding*. He had no trouble recognizing the company name and knocked as loudly as he could on the tempered glass. The reception area was weekend-empty, but light was coming from around the corner. He had to knock three times and yell "Security" before his polo-shirted quarry came to the door of Roanoke Engineering and Development. Rick Chase,

Consulting Engineer, was the fourth name down.

"How did you know—" Rick began, after opening the door, but Robert interrupted, "I called security and asked if you'd checked in." He omitted the part about the distraught parishioner.

"Since you didn't have the courtesy to come to the special vestry meeting this morning, you probably haven't heard that Clare, the women hit by the tower stone, has died."

Rick looked from side to side. "No ... well, yes, I knew from—"

"Oh, sure, from Ms. O'Reilly of KORN TV," Robert interrupted again. "All the more reason you should have been at the meeting. I could have used your help today, Rick. I'm convinced that the stone didn't fall, but was thrown out of the tower; it will take an engineer to prove it. We need a liaison to coordinate with the police and the city and our insurers and whoever else wants to stick their noses in."

"Father Robert, I'd be glad—"

"No Rick, I'm sure you won't have the time since you're working weekends on this big project." Robert walked over to the table holding the architectural plans. "Great name. Church Square Development." He made no effort to turn back the large pages. "Let me guess: there'll be a multi-story condo, boutique shops, a private garden no one knows is a burial place, and a big fence surrounding the whole thing, including the church. I guess we'll have to issue the congregation picture IDs so they can come to services."

The younger man was hanging his head.

"It's funny, son, people are always saying that churches should be run like businesses, aiming for profit and prosperity. Now, of course, we need to be good stewards of what God has given us. I just wish that people could see the beauty of the Jesus Christ business model."

Voice raised to preaching level, Robert elaborated, "In his model, returns on investment don't go into the bank, or fund the CEO's year-end bonus. No, they go right back into the business of feeding, clothing and housing the needy, and providing a place for worship. The more that gets given away, the better Jesus likes it. If I were a Baptist I could quote you chapter and verse from the Gospel, but I think you get my drift."

Robert paused, and his voice softened. "Now, Rick, I'm sure that our half block could benefit from some responsible development. For instance, rent from those top floor condo's could subsidize the food bank located down below. And proceeds from the rental of church property would sure help with building maintenance, not to mention the tower repair."

Robert walked toward Rick, who had backed himself into the corner. "What you're planning here turns the church and the grounds into a theme park. I know you're capable of putting together a package that would be more in tune with our Lord's business model, but I think you've been seduced by what I'd call more worldly concerns." .

"Father," Rick said, "believe me, I would never—"

"I know you wouldn't plan to benefit directly, Rick. I know you were raised a Christian, and I also know that you're well aware of the various conflict of interest statues. But I doubt your business partner, whoever she or he is, has the same scruples."

Rick was struggling mightily to answer, but Robert didn't stay to listen. "Think about what I've said, son," he said at the door. "Come to church on Sunday and pray about it. God be with you." And like the church's caped crusader, he vanished.

After taxiing back up the hill, Robert quickly convened his meeting. They met yet again in the church sanctuary.

Robert began, "After this business is over, I'm canceling all meetings for six months. And this one will be quick. Our goal is to make the Bishop think we've removed Clare's memorial without actually removing it. I could just refuse outright, but I'm tired of all this confrontation. Let's figure out a creative solution."

"You mean a sneaky solution, don't you?" mumbled Mary. For this gathering her food offering was sticks of red licorice, with a few black ones thrown in for Joe.

"Now you're talking my language," chimed in Lester, "and I've had an inspiration. See, someone throws a blanket over the big guy when he gets out of his car and hustles him right by the display and into the church. Me and my buddies will stand lookout in front to make sure no one interferes. You can tell that Bishop he's a big shot and needs protection. There's your answer and if I wasn't feeling so generous right now my inspiration would cost you a bundle."

Joe countered, "and while we're at it, let's kidnap him on his way out and hold him for ransom. I figure 50K should cover the tower repair."

"I'll keep my disdain to myself until I get outside," Lester growled, "but I sure hope I don't run into your little pipsqueak of a car, that Mini-Coupette. I may not be able to control my temperature."

"Wait a minute, that's my Mini-Cooper, too," Mary piped in. "Calm down, Les. Joe's just jealous he didn't think of your solution first."

"That's right, Joe said. "Look, before we go any further, I need to report on whose ashes we found the other day."

"You've found out already? Way to go!" Robert stood up on one foot and clapped Joe on the shoulder.

Lucy's glum expression turned animated. "That's wonderful! Was it one of our organists? Which one? Wait, I'm sure I know. It must have been Tim Evans. I don't know how he died or how he came to be here, but it must be him. Everyone at Heritage House remembers what a nice man he was. Just the sort of man who would put red laces on his organ shoes for AIDS awareness. That idea came from my niece Lisa, who wears pink laces for breast cancer awareness. It must be him. I just know it!"

Joe interjected, "Thanks for making my report for me, Lucy. Now don't blush, your intuition is spot on. I'll just add a few more details."

He stood up and raised his arm as if holding a pointer. "I've been helping Robert locate Tim Evan's whereabouts, with help from Lucy's brother Thomas. After Tim left suddenly for Minnesota to bury his former partner, Henry thought he'd seen the last of him. That accounted for his surprise when the box of ashes and shoes were uncovered at Neola's burial. He recognized the shoes as belonging to Tim."

Waving the invisible pointer back and forth, he continued, "I did a bit of sleuthing and found out that Tim died of AIDS soon after he arrived in Minneapolis. After that, his remains were transferred to a Seattle funeral home. Not only his ashes, but his organist's shoes with their red laces."

Robert raised his hand. "Is packing shoes in with ashes some sort of ritual I haven't heard about?"

"That's a good one, Robert. No, Tim probably intended for his shoes to be cremated also, but for some reason, it didn't happen. The funeral home changed hands after Tim's ashes arrived, but the new owners verified that they were delivered to Grace church and on what date. It was before you arrived, Robert. I'll follow up with your secretary and Henry on everyone's whereabouts at the time."

Mary swallowed her last bite of her licorice and said, "Joe's already asked me about the dates, although I'm not sure why he bothered. He knows how memory-challenged I am." She had entered the main aisle and was practicing hefting the big Gospel book over her head, as directed by the bishop for Sunday's service.

Following the big book with his eyes, Robert said, "A final question, in two parts. How did that big crate get in the ground without anyone knowing, and who would be clueless enough to put it there?"

Lester muttered, "Like a cowboy being buried with his boots on."

After fifteen more minutes of futile discussion about how to deal with Clare's memorial, everyone was frustrated. Then Daniel, who until now had appeared fully preoccupied practicing his keyboarding on top of the pew, said, "Uh, I have an idea. It came to me because we're sitting here in the church and I've been practicing one of tomorrow's hymns, the one that starts, 'If thou but trust.' It was written in the 1600s, just after Martin Luther and King Henry and the others had stood up to the Pope. Everyone was composing new hymns; that's why the hymnal's so thick. That and the fact that now it also includes some Jewish hymns, like the Torah song the kids are doing tomorrow."

"Daniel, you can pack more information covering more centuries in two minutes than anyone I know." said Robert. "Your idea is—?"

Daniel answered, "I know, it's time to get to the point. Here it is. The whole first line of the hymn goes, 'If thou but trust in God to guide thee.' There's a lot after that, but it gave me the idea that we should pray for an answer instead of depending on just ourselves."

Silence reigned.

"That's it?" asked Robert. "What a creative, might I say, divinely inspired suggestion. I propose we proceed with haste."

After fifteen minutes of silent and spoken prayer, including a short soliloquy by Lester and ending with the Lord's Prayer, Lucy sighed. "Out of the mouths of babes. Daniel, you are the sweetest young man. I only wish you and my niece were closer in age. You'd be perfect for each other."

Daniel looked up, eyes wide. "Your niece who plays the organ? Oh, I'd like to be perfect for her. But I wouldn't be. You're about the first friends I've had other than my mom and my teachers, and all of you are old. Only older people seem to like me, and little kids. It's awfully nice of you to think of me, though."

"Lucy, how old is Lisa?" asked Mary.

"Oh dear, only sixteen. Wait, that was before the silly argument that caused my estrangement from Lisa and her father. My heavens, she can't be eighteen?"

"Daniel has just turned twenty five and would probably be more comfortable with a younger person—no offense, dear," said Mary. "I'd say that's close enough in age, wouldn't you all? Daniel, don't worry; we won't play matchmaker, beyond introducing you to Lisa tomorrow after the service. You've already met her father Thomas the other night here in the church."

Daniel smiled. "Maybe after the service she'd like to hear me play some of the variations on the postlude. Father Robert said I could only play one variation at the service, but I've practiced them all."

Lucy beamed. "I'm sure she'd be thrilled, and would you like to join Lisa, Thomas and me for brunch after the service? My treat."

Daniel nodded vigorously.

"Good, that's settled," said Robert. "Now I'll tell you how my prayer was answered. Here's how we'll handle Clare's memorial pile so the Bishop won't suspect a thing."

◌਼

After leaving the church, Lester met up with Pete under the freeway. His buddy had been watching over Lester's backpack and bedroll and Spike, who barked a welcome.

"Where are you bedding down?" Lester asked.

Pete threw his pack over his shoulder. "The United Tribes just opened a new shelter in Pioneer Square. Thought I'd try it out. If you put on a bandanna I could probably sneak you in. We could leave Spike with one of the guys."

"Na." Lester locked Spike in a bear hug. "I've been neglecting my buddy. I think I'll take him up to the off leash dog run, then bed down here. We've got to be back at the church early for security detail."

"Okay, later." The two bumped fists and Pete started off down the hill.

Chapter 8

The rain ended just before dawn on Sunday, March 27th. Drops fell from the church roof and burst like miniature water balloons on the pavement. Mist blanketed the garden. As it dispersed over the next hour, the roses, daisies and carnations on Clare's memorial were revealed in their crimson, canary and turquoise-dyed glory.

The answer to Robert's prayer had been to transform the memorial into a temporary reception area for the Bishop. Soon after the mist lifted, Lester and his crew of panhandling friends joined the ladies of the altar guild in dividing the flower offerings into bunches for distribution to the children who would be attending the service. Henry stashed the bagged offerings of birdseed in plastic bins so they could carry on with Clare's work. Mrs. Peters and the guild ladies showed Lester and company how to fashion the remaining stray flowers into garlands, which they placed over the stray bits of soggy birdseed.

"Now if I can just locate the Christmas tree lights," Mrs. Peters told Lester, "We'll string them over the rhododendrons as the *pièce de résistance*."

Lester squinted, rubbed his ear, and asked, "The PS duh what?"

Lucy had been deputized by Father Robert to organize the children into a welcoming committee. They were to jump up and down the minute the Bishop appeared, the better to hide the still messy garden.

Father Robert had also prevailed upon one of Clare's mourners, another pigeon lover, to lure the birds away during the critical hours of the Bishop's visit with some of the donated birdseed. Sporting a T-shirt emblazoned with a red pigeon over his clerical shirt—part of the memorabilia left at the memorial—he watched the relocation maneuvers with admiration. Henry swept up after the flock as it fluttered down the street. It was probably too much to hope that an albino specimen would stay behind to represent the Holy Spirit.

"Mary," he called to his deacon, who was handing out coffee and donuts, "remind me to take off this shirt before the Bishop gets here."

∽

Two others who weren't church members or volunteers had arrived early that morning. One of them, Seattle police officer Joyce Hitchcock, was sitting in her cruiser across the street from the church and noticed the stranger immediately. Father Robert hadn't asked her to come; he didn't need to. Over the past week she'd spent quite a bit of time at the church investigating the discovery of the unidentified ashes and the incident that had led to Clare's death.

She didn't expect trouble today, not really, but darn it, she liked these folks. She liked how they called her "Officer Joyce" and weren't intimidated by her uniform and towering height. And besides, this was part of her patrol district and calls were few and far between on Sunday mornings. She also hoped for an opportunity to fraternize with Officer Chen after his off-duty job providing security for the food bank. Maybe he'd be here again today.

She zeroed in on the second stranger, who was standing

next to the curb. Medium height, medium age, tan pants and jacket, tennis shoes, and a baseball cap tilted over his eyes. He was carrying something that looked like a salesman's sample case. Dressed too neatly for a street person and too casually for a churchgoer. Despite the bland appearance, he seemed familiar to Joyce.

As a black Lincoln Town Car approached the curb, she saw him stiffen and move forward. It looked like the sort of car a church bigwig might drive. Joyce grabbed the door handle of her cruiser.

Before she could act, the man stepped back and an elderly couple alighted, followed by three children. A woman she recognized from the church ran forward and escorted the children to the garden. The man seemed to lose interest, and Joyce sank back into her seat.

Five minutes later a blue sedan zipped in front of the Lincoln and screeched to a halt in the delivery zone. A compact, well-barbered man in his sixties wearing a black suit and purple shirt exited, dragging a long staff behind him. A red-coated woman emerged next, carrying a garment bag. Seeing the waiting children, the man held his staff aloft and shouted, "Suffer the little children to come unto me!"

What the hell? Joyce wondered.

❦

Lucy whispered loudly to the children, "You're on," and the welcome began. The little ones performed as directed, surrounding His Grace completely in a jumping, swirling mass. Stray flowers flew in all directions. Father Robert, T-shirt removed, signaled to the head usher, who was standing at the door of the church. She disappeared inside, and a minute later, loud chimes clanged, produced by Daniel from the organ console.

CR

The stranger had made his way to the edge of the group around the bishop and was attempting to penetrate the writhing sea of children by pushing their little shoulders aside when Officer Joyce tapped him on the shoulder.

"Excuse me, sir," she said. "I suggest you stand back."

The man turned around, looked up at her stern face, and gave a start. Lowering the brim of his hat, he mumbled, "I'm trying to speak to the bishop before the service starts. I have something important to tell him."

"It can wait," Joyce answered. "Instead of interrupting the festivities, I suggest you call and make an appointment. Or, if it's that important, wait until the coffee hour after the service."

"You don't understand!" the man exclaimed. "By then that Father will have a chance to sweet-talk the bishop out of what's rightfully ours!"

"Be that as it may," Joyce answered, wishing she could pull the man's cap off to make an ID, "I'm telling you to wait, and I'm staying by your side to make sure you do. And by the way, you'll need to remove your hat in the church. Those are the rules."

The stranger glared at her as he backed away toward one of the stone benches that lined the garden courtyard. The three kindergarteners standing on its seat kindly and gently pushed him forward. Their touch sent his arms flying up and out in an attempt to maintain his balance. The case that he'd been carrying flew away, and he leapt over the children to retrieve it. The children ran every which-way to avoid him but then surrounded him as he lay on the ground, clutching the case to his chest. They shook their fingers at him as one of them chanted, "You're a bad man!" The rest added their voices. "You're a bad man. You're a bad man!"

"You're a lucky man, Robert," the Bishop called to the rector over the children's heads ten minutes later. "You've got some dead benefactors who wanted to save this pile of rubble. A special delivery letter from an attorney came in late yesterday. I'll give you the scoop while we tour the facilities before the service."

The bishop continued, "Great idea I had to take the kids along. We'll get their advice on improvements to the Sunday school rooms and lavatories. Now that you're off the hook for repairs, you'd be wise to put most of that bequest where it will return the most on investment." As Robert stood open-mouthed, the Bishop raised his staff in the air and shouted, "This way, little lambs!" and turned toward the parish hall, the tour's first stop.

The flock swept Lucy Lawrence and Deacon Mary along with them. Robert stood his ground and cut off the two women as they reached his side. "Did you hear what Bishop Anthony said?" he asked.

"I heard the word 'benefactors,' " said Mary. "That sounds promising."

"And I heard 'attorney,' said Lucy. "That implies a will."

"But who … who would have … who *had* enough money to—" Robert tapped his temple with his fingers. Then he broke into a grin and gave a little hop on his good foot. "Can you guess?" he asked the women.

"I can," chortled Mary.

"I think I can," breathed Lucy.

Robert hobbled into the parish hall to join the entourage, circling round the kids to join the Bishop. He leaned over and spoke a few words in his superior's ear. Bishop Anthony nodded and shouted, "Right off the block! How'd you guess?"

"Well, the net assets of the rest of the people I've buried

in the past year couldn't total over a few grand," Robert answered. "Isn't it a little soon, though? In my experience, it can take years to settle an estate."

"I don't know, and I don't really care," answered Bishop Anthony. "What I'm concerned about right now is the condition of these floors. When was the last time they were varnished?"

"Just one more question," Robert interrupted. "Can I announce that we received the bequest during the service?"

"As long as you wait until after my sermon," the bishop cautioned. "I hate having my thunder stolen."

Seeing Mary and Lucy at the back of the hall, Robert gave the high sign. Their jumping and squealing inspired the children, who followed suit.

The Bishop pounded his staff on the floor for order, but Robert was oblivious. He was reminiscing. Those dear folks had loved Grace Church. He just hadn't realized how much. They'd also been fond of Clare, admiring the woman's obsession with feeding God's flock of pigeons. When the more stuffy members of the parish had complained about the mess, they had defended her presence in the church courtyard. How fitting that their bequest had come at this moment.

To further delight him, Molly appeared at his side, and they sauntered along together behind the Bishop. After ten steps, she brought him back to earth with a soft but crisply spoken statement. "Robert, I've been thinking about what you told me about the problems involved when a priest has a ... *relationship* with a parishioner. Despite my flip answer the other day about your turning me away at the church door, I do understand your predicament. But what if the priest began seeing this person while this person was attending another church? And what if the priest gradually let it be known to his congregation that he was dating this person? He could escort her to a few functions—oh, let's see, the parish picnic or the visiting chorus from California—just so people could look her over, so to speak. And then, if the relationship started becoming, ah, serious, wouldn't the parish expect that she might start attending the priest's church? And from there, well—"

The Bishop's baritone would have interrupted a full choir singing the Hallelujah Chorus. "On to the Sunday School rooms!"

Robert just smiled at Molly and nodded vigorously.

രൂ

Rick Chase, wearing his meet-with-investors gray-striped suit, stood at the edge of the throng swirling around the Bishop. Most of the rest of the vestry were there also and had exchanged thumbs-ups when the Bishop announced the bequest. After a moment's hesitation, he joined them.

He'd left the office yesterday soon after Father Robert, feeling the need to be in a neutral place. The shame he'd felt as Robert spoke about the rightful beneficiaries of church property development had turned to anger five minutes after his rector had departed in a cloud of virtue.

Flipping through the pages of the Church Square Development plan, he thought, *Damn it, this had the potential to be a groundbreaking project, a win-win for the church and the investors. It would attract residents to the area more likely to attend church, and that would build up the congregation, producing more dollars in the collection plate.* And what about the tasteful arts center he'd envisioned on the ground floor of the condo, along with a branch of his favorite coffee shop? He and his partner Cliff had even discussed submitting the new building for LEED certification, and if that wasn't virtuous, he didn't know what was.

But then, looking down at the site plan, he saw the cross hatches designating the wrought-iron fence surrounding the property. He imagined a parishioner, wanting to pray in the sanctuary on a weekday morning, shaking the locked gates. Gazing at the north section, he imagined a poor mother of three getting off the bus with her children, shepherding them to the food bank entry, only to see the sign saying it was closed. She would have to find her way ten blocks south to an old warehouse next to the waste incinerator.

After driving around aimlessly for a while, Rick decided to go home and talk to Stacy. After all, she was the one who'd gotten him into this mess by insisting that they get married at Grace church. Thereafter she'd left him alone most Sunday mornings until he gave up and went to services with her—unless there was a good game on TV. He'd fallen in love with the Stone Gothic building and its garden. He'd even found himself wondering if it was a sacrilege to say your prayers to an arched column or a stained glass window.

Stacy, once she recovered from her shock at hearing about the project—How long was he planning to avoid telling her, she asked, right up until the wrecking ball smashed the rectory?—had him describe his meeting with Father Robert from beginning to end.

She then pointed out that Father Robert hadn't said he didn't want *any* development, just a change in beneficiaries from downtown investors to the existing community—the parishioners, the pigeon ladies, the food bank users and all the rest.

"You can even have your double Americanos on-site at your precious coffee shop," she told him, "as long as the food bank customers can use donated coupons to join you." She said a lot of other things, too, and he hadn't slept well at all last night. He hoped—prayed, actually—that she would agree to sit next to him at the upcoming service.

Now Rick Chase skirted the crowd and left the building, cell phone to his ear. "Hey, Cliff, sorry, but the deal's off. They've found another investor."

Chapter 9

The 10:30 service was due to begin in fifteen minutes, and the best pew spots in front were filled. Any latecomers would have to lean around the huge pillars supporting the 1902 structure in order to follow the proceedings. If they knew the truth of it, they might have stayed away altogether. The last of the engineers to evaluate the sanctuary had described the walls as "a pile of rubble, temporarily vertical." It seemed that the church elders in the early years of the twentieth century had decided against the newfangled practice of using iron structural beams for support.

The church ordinarily had two main points of entry, but the one leading from the Memorial Garden was still ringed with hazard tape. So Lucy Lawrence stood at the north entrance, waiting for her brother and niece. She'd called Lisa the night before, asking the young organ-prodigy to befriend Daniel. She needn't have bothered. Lisa knew all about the new organist at Grace Church through the young musicians' grapevine.

"I hear he has soulful brown eyes," Lisa enthused, "and gorgeous curly hair."

In the interest of full disclosure, Lucy described his eccentric communication style.

"Oh, lots of musicians come up short in the social graces department," Lisa laughed. "We're so obsessive, you know."

Lucy smoothed the skirt of her new blue suit, feeling a bit self-conscious. She realized she hadn't been paying much attention to her appearance recently, preferring to cover up with her trench coat. She'd been feeling old and useless, estranged from her family and losing too many friends like Neola. Strangely, even though the past week had brought Neola's funeral and Clare's death, each day she helped reveal the identity of the mysterious ashes and supported Father Robert in his efforts to keep the parish alive and thriving had made her feel more vigorous.

After lifting each foot in turn to check for mud spots on her matching pumps, Lucy scanned the crowd, looking for her brother and Lisa. There was that nice policewoman Officer Hitchcock approaching … or was it Officer Joyce? Wouldn't it be wonderful if she joined the church? It would probably be the first time that someone was evangelized as the result of a murder investigation.

Officer Joyce approached Lucy. "Nice blue suit, Ma'am. The exact same color as my cruiser. Say, do you see that fellow over there, standing next to the big marble bowl?"

Lucy turned to look. "Oh, you mean the baptismal font?"

"Yes, the font," said Joyce. Do you think the usher could put him somewhere where I can keep an eye on him? And tell him to take off his hat?"

Lucy started to ask why, and then took another look at the man, who seemed familiar. He was medium height and wore a tan windbreaker. Dressed more for bowling than for church. Where had she seen him before?

"I know just the place." With a smile, Lucy walked over to one of the ushers, and they consulted for a moment. The man nodded, moved to the baptismal font, and gestured the man forward. The man seemed willing to go, even pointing toward the front, as if wanting to get as close as possible.

Joyce waved at the usher and mouthed, "His hat, his

hat! Tell him to take off his hat." She pointed to her own head.

But the usher was doing everything at his own stately pace. It seemed to take him five minutes to lead the man to his seat. When they arrived, the usher bowed deeply toward the altar. Only then did he turn and motion to the man to remove his cap. The man shook his head. The usher clicked his black-shoed feet together and placed his white-gloved hand on the pew back.

Joyce could feel the chill of the usher's glare from the back of the church. After a few seconds, the man whipped the cap off and hurried to the far end of the pew.

Of course, Joyce thought. She should have been able to ID him with the hat on; her training had certainly taught her that much. But even experts have off days, she supposed.

She turned to Lucy. "Ms. Lawrence, take a look … do you recognize him?"

"Why, yes, and I'm surprised he's here today. Now, let me tell you why I decided on that particular pew." Lucy chuckled. "It's impossible to exit from the far end. See the column that's in the way? For the past hundred years mothers have seated their rambunctious children in that pew. That's the reason it's the only one still empty; it gives the regular attendees claustrophobia."

Lucy pointed Officer Joyce to a seat behind the man and checked her watch. It was almost time for the service to begin, and where were her brother and niece? Just then, Lisa and Thomas arrived. Her brother announced breathlessly, "Your niece put on and discarded three outfits before I insisted we leave. It must be a new phase."

Lisa, elegant in her vintage green velvet suit, smiled at her aunt, and Lucy smiled back.

It was time for the opening procession and hymn. Per the bishop's instructions, Robert had managed to find four acolytes of approximately the same height: a gangly teenage boy, the star forward for the women's basketball team, another tall man in dreadlocks, and Joe, who looked at sea dressed in a white robe and carrying a candle. Old George, the crucifer, was in the lead, accompanied discreetly by a shorter acolyte who scooted behind him, righting the swaying cross when it listed too far to the right or left. Then came the choir. It hadn't been possible to right-size them, because they ranged in age from sixteen to ninety-two, and one was being pushed in a wheelchair.

Deacon Mary came next, struggling mightily to keep the huge Gospel book aloft.

Father Robert hobbled behind her, resplendent in the gold velveteen stole made by the Sunday School, its fabric splashed with the multi-colored prints of small hands. He had inserted two more candle-bearing acolytes—identical fourteen-year-old twins—behind him and in front of the bishop, to minimize their clashing vestment colors.

Molly Ferguson arranged the Bishop's long robe behind him before he started forward, waving and smiling from side to side at the congregation. He carried the large staff in his left hand. In his raised right hand was a gold item called an aspergillum, which resembled the sprinkler bottle women used years ago when ironing. He flicked it at those unlucky enough to be in his sights with large blobs of water. It was his favorite way of blessing people. "It wakes them up, gets them involved!" he liked to say.

As the procession was halfway up the aisle to the tune of "Lift High the Cross," an aid car with siren blaring passed the church on its way up the hill to the hospital. The wail of the siren was punctuated by the banging of the radiators lining the walls as they filled with steam. Daniel, used to commotions such as this, deftly segued from hymn tune to interlude and back again. The Bishop, having arrived at the altar steps, tried to shout the opening sentences of the liturgy over the din.

"THE LORD BE WITH YOU!"

The children's little hands clamped over their ears. One precocious Sunday-schooler shouted back, "YOU'RE FUNNY!"

The service lurched forward from there, and after climbing the pulpit to preach the sermon, the Bishop continued to shout, this time into a live microphone. He seemed to have forgotten his planned children's sermon, instead launching into a series of rhetorical questions. "WHO IS IT WHO LIGHTS UP THE SKY?" he thundered.

Into the silence, a tremulous voice from the other side of the altar interjected, "It's him!"

The Bishop either didn't hear or chose to ignore the interruption, bellowing, "WHO IS IT, I SAY? "

"It's him!" came the answer.

"That's what I like, a fervent seeker after the Lord!" proclaimed His Grace, turning toward Daniel, who had walked from the organ console to the lectern opposite the pulpit. "Speak out, son; don't be afraid to say His name. WHO IS THE JUDGE OF US ALL?"

"I'm sorry, but I don't know his name," Daniel answered.

At that point the service came to a screeching halt. None of this was in the service bulletin.

Pointing to the third row, Daniel announced, "*He* was in the mirror I use to see what's going on behind me when I'm playing. It's the man who was in the church tower after Miss Clare was hit by the stone."

Daniel's eyes widened. "Now I remember! It's Miss Neola's son-in-law, the one who got so mad when the sexton dug up the box of ashes in her burial plot. Why would he be in a tower throwing stones?"

"That's what I'd like to know," said Officer Joyce from her fourth row pew.

All present turned toward the third row right, as Mark

Miller, Neola Peterson's son-in law, shouted, "It wasn't my fault that lady was there when I … when the stone fell! This place is possessed, and the devil wants to turn my wife's inheritance into filthy lucre!" He held up the bag he was carrying. "And watch out when I let loose what's in here!"

He turned and tried to escape from the end of his row as screams arose from the surrounding pew occupants who had heard him. When he couldn't fit around the column blocking his exit, he climbed up and over the pew, into the waiting arms of Officer Joyce. More sirens whooped and hollered from the street outside, and the radiators banged in reply as she escorted the struggling man from the church.

As she hustled Mark out the door, she yelled, "Stay right where you are, everyone. That's an order! Whatever he's got in his bag is going outside with us."

The Bishop, recognizing a fellow take-charge person, echoed her through the microphone, "STAY RIGHT WHERE YOU ARE."

Daniel ran back to his organ and launched into the interlude he'd scheduled after the finish of the Bishop's sermon. This helped to calm the congregation. It also effectively shortened the sermon by fifteen minutes.

଼

Once outside, Joyce called for backup with her free hand, using her one-arm restraint technique to keep Mark Miller's hand up toward his shoulder. Joe, who had followed her outside, white robe flapping, grabbed the satchel, hustled to the opposite side of the garden, and put it down carefully.

"Officer Chen, what are you doing here?" Joyce asked, seeing her colleague from Neola's funeral standing on the sidewalk.

"I thought I'd provide a little informal security for the big event," he answered, tipping his police baseball cap. "A good idea, no?" he added, as he placed hazard tape around the satchel, to the accompaniment of the interlude music floating out the open church doors.

଼

The congregation had settled somewhat, but there was a good deal of shifting and murmuring as the Bishop spoke at the beginning of the announcement period.

"Listen up, people," he said loudly, having turned off the microphone. "I've got some good news for you. Some benefactors have left their estate to your building fund. That should help shore up that tower of yours, and maybe leave some extra for a bigger cross on top."

He pulled a piece of paper from his voluminous robe. "Neola? Strange name. That's the name of your benefactor. Let's see, it says here that she and her predeceased husband Fred's estate will go to Grace church 'so long as the church uses the funds for restoration. If not,' she says, 'I reluctantly bequeath everything to my ungrateful daughter, my spoiled grandchildren, and my daughter's crazy new husband.' I assume that's the fellow who was escorted out," the Bishop deduced, and then paused. One of the elderly ushers proceeded slowly up the steps to the altar area, turned left, and continued up the spiral staircase to the pulpit where the Bishop stood.

The congregation resumed their murmuring. It was unheard of for someone other than the preacher to enter the pulpit, especially when the preacher was the Bishop.

Nevertheless, the gentleman was standing there, bowing, which was difficult in the cramped space. He then leaned down to whisper into the shorter man's ear. Bishop Anthony nodded and raised his hand to bless the man, connecting painfully with the usher's nose. The man descended the stairs in all due haste as Bishop Anthony

131

announced, "My friend here has been advised by the police that they have identified the item, er, *items*, in the satchel of the man who was arrested. You will be able to safely exit the building." Seeing the panic on the faces before him, he hastened to add, "It's not, ah, what you might suspect. It was—" For once, Bishop Anthony Adams seemed to be at a loss for words.

He beckoned Father Robert to his side. It took a minute for Robert to thump over in his walking cast and navigate the winding stairs. The solid oak pulpit of Grace church was as grand as the altar and stained glass windows. Bishop Anthony then whispered in the rector's ear for at least a minute.

Robert, swaying a little due to his cramped position, addressed the congregation, who by this time were leaning forward in expectation. "Dear friends, this isn't the sort of statement usually made from the pulpit, but please bear with me. We think the man escorted out of the church may be the one who dropped, or threw, the tower stone that resulted in Ms. Clare's death. I'm sorry I don't know her last name, but many of you know her as The Pigeon Lady.

"There will have to be an investigation, of course, but suffice to say that this man came to the church to cause trouble with what he referred to as his 'secret weapon.' "

Robert began to laugh. "Excuse me, but, you see, he works as a pest exterminator and thought what he had in his satchel would do the job. His satchel contained," he paused to compose himself, "three large, ugly rats that he'd trapped at his last job."

"Rats?"

"Did he say there are rats?"

"One hundred rats?"

Various members of the already jittery congregation started to make their way toward the exit, starting a stampede from the pews.

"Wait, stop! The rats are *outside*, not in here!" Robert

yelled, prompting greater chaos.

Just then, a wall of sound descended on the throng, loud and soothing at the same time. It consisted of chimes interspersed with ethereal chords, then the beginning line of a familiar hymn tune, "Now the silence, now the peace ... "

"Miraculous," Robert whispered, as the flow toward the doors ebbed and everyone began returning to the pews. Once again, Daniel and his organ had saved the day.

CR

Twenty minutes later, after Holy Eucharist had been administered, the service seemed to be approaching an end. Daniel did his part by omitting the second-to-the-last hymn. All that was left was the final blessing by the bishop, this one from the high altar and without water.

Instead, in yet another departure from protocol, Anthony Adams strode to the same lectern where Daniel had stood earlier to identify Mark Miller. He grabbed Robert's sleeve as he went to pull him along. A collective sigh ascended from the congregation.

During their march to the lectern, the Bishop said, sotto voce and with mic off, "I missed my chance, Bob. I should have tried casting out the demon from Mr. Miller, like Jesus did in Mark 1:21."

Robert gaped, then whooped.

"This is the best time I've ever had on a visitation," The Bishop said. "Are all your services like this?"

"No, Bishop Anthony, only when you're visiting," said Robert.

At the lectern, placing his arm around the rector's shoulders, the Bishop asked one final rhetorical question. "Do you folks think you can manage to keep this place going and growing during the tower restoration?"

Robert reached for the microphone, which the Bishop

handed to him, and looked out over the pews. "Let's answer with the commitment phrase from our prayer book: Will you, the members of Grace Church, do all in your power to support this community as we rebuild in memory of Neola, Fred, Clare, and all the saints who've gone before ... to the glory of God?"

"WE WILL!" shouted the congregation.

Chapter 10

The service for Clare was held the following Tuesday in the Memorial Garden, in deference to the many mourners, including her pigeons, who wouldn't be comfortable inside the church. Pete, Lester's buddy, began the proceedings with ceremonial drumming. Then Lester delivered the eulogy, having received a special commission from Father Robert. From observing the Bishop the previous Sunday, Lester had learned the value of brevity, and kept his remarks short and subdued.

After Lester's last Amen, Father Robert told the crowd, "Today we have not one, but three internments. First, one of our parishioners, Lucy Lawrence, has generously purchased and donated a plot to receive Clare's ashes."

Lucy, standing next to her brother Thomas and niece Lisa, blushed at the applause.

"In addition," Robert continued, "Neola's ashes are being laid to rest in her original plot, next to her husband Fred's. Her daughter Audrey sends her appreciation to all of you and regrets that other obligations keep her away today.

"Lastly, our former organist Tim's ashes are also being re-interred, along with the red laces from his organ shoes, which I've decided are organic and therefore acceptable for burial. I've given Tim's shoes to his friend, Henry, and asked him to say a few words."

Henry, dressed in a shiny gray suit borrowed from old George the crucifer, stepped forward.

"Before he left here so suddenly," Henry began, "Tim told me that he was beholden to the folks at Grace Church, because they'd treated a sick man with dignity. He especially mentioned me in that respect." With a look that dared anyone to contradict him, Henry continued, "Tim Evans may have been a pansy, but he treated me no different than the rector or the big shots of the parish, unlike a few others I could name. And like I told Joe here, he'd play any instrument on the organ I asked him to." Henry began to cry.

Father Robert turned to Joe, who took over. "Henry here was on vacation when Mr. Evan's ashes were transferred to Grace church for burial—that was five years ago, before Father Robert came, and the church was between rectors. The person filling in must not have known that only cremains are to be placed in the garden and that these should be removed from the container. He put everything, including the shoes, in a crate and buried it all. It ended up filling Neola Peterson's plot as well as Tim's."

Henry spoke up, "Why wasn't it discovered when the landscapers took off the topsoil awhile back?"

"The landscapers only removed six inches worth of soil, not enough to uncover the crate. I went to some trouble to verify that, since there was so much concern about the rest of the cremains being trucked to the landfill." He added, "I'm sorry, everyone, for the undignified words. But to finish, the fill-in priest also removed the identification from the box, probably to make sure the name on the memorial plaque would be correct. But then the nameplate was never ordered. So the only record of Tim's burial is in an old ledger I located in the basement archives."

"Don't forget to mention why the shoes had red laces," said Lisa, who was standing between her aunt Lucy and Daniel. "It's the same reason I wear pink laces on my organists' shoes, in memory of my Mom who died of breast cancer. I'll bet Tim was remembering all the people who've died from AIDS. Don't you think so, Daniel? Daniel?"

Daniel, who had been standing beside her, was now walking toward the other side of the garden. He would have bumped into Father Robert if the priest hadn't stepped aside. A slender, middle-aged man with gray curly hair and brown eyes, dressed in a shaggy sweater, stepped forward.

"Hello, son," he said.

"Hello, Dad," Daniel answered.

⚛

After the funeral, Robert invited a few people over to the rectory to celebrate Daniel's reunion with his father. When everyone was settled in the living room with snacks and drinks, Robert asked Molly, who'd served as the Bishop's representative at the service, if she'd like to tour the rectory.

"What do you think of my cozy abode?" he asked after the tour, as they descended the three flights of bare wood stairs. "I'm rather proud of the shelf system I designed for my Mad Magazine collection."

Molly, dressed in a red tunic and black slacks, put her hand to her ear. "What? I can't hear you over the squeaking of these stairs. Robert, I hate to be a snob, but I guess I can't help it. You've done your best, and this place is still falling apart. If it were me, I'd refuse to live right next door to the church, a block above a noisy freeway, and sleep in an attic where I have to look through iron window bars while I wash the dishes. It would be too depressing to see the folks lined up for the food bank and pigeons flying all around."

The stairs creaked some more as Robert shifted his weight to the foot closest to Molly, which luckily was the one without a cast. "Beggars can't be choosers," he said. "I've always lived in rectories and taken in boarders for company.

Um, where do you live, Molly?"

"My home is only three miles away, next to a greenbelt. No pigeons, but lots of crows and woodpeckers. It has vaulted ceilings and lots of glass, and a daylight basement that has room for all types of … collections. My husband and I were very happy there, and I'd never leave. But it's lonely now. At least you've had Daniel to keep you company, but that will probably end soon."

They remained on the stair landing, talking.

Ω

In the living room, the group was discussing the latest developments in the criminal case against Neola's son in law. Mark Miller had been released from jail on his own recognizance.

Joe was speaking. "Our friend Officer Joyce told me his blood pressure was so high when he was arrested that they were afraid he'd have a stroke. They put him on house arrest, meaning he can only go as far as the trash can and back. I'll bet he wishes he were anywhere else. Neola's daughter must be making his life a living hell since she found out what hubby had been up to. That's probably why she didn't attend her mother's internment today."

"Speaking of 'up to,' " Lucy said, "why did he throw those stones from the tower? Surely he wasn't intent on murder. And how was he able to get up there?"

Mary answered, "He'd run up a lot of debt on a side business without telling his family. He'd banked on the inheritance from his in-laws to cover it. After the funeral he learned that all of Neola and Fred's bequest would be going to the church. He was so desperate that his self-righteous, holier-than-thou personality cracked."

Mary looked at Joe. "How did he get up in the tower?"

Joe looked around. "Is Henry here?" Seeing no sign of

the sexton, he continued, "Mark Miller saw the exterior door to the tower when Henry took it upon himself to give him a tour of the church perimeter after the burial. The door was fastened with a simple chain and padlock that it took you, Lester, only a few seconds to disable so you could go up to watch the sunset."

Seeing that Lester was about to elaborate at length, Joe intervened, "Let me tell the condensed version. If anyone wants to hear the full story they can talk to you later.

"Now Lester always made sure the chain was locked after he came down, but all Mr. Miller needed were some bolt cutters to release it. I don't think he had intended to do anything other than look around, but when he saw the extra stones lying on the tower floor, he couldn't resist the temptation. You realize he'd seen the stone fall at his mother-in-law's internment. He must have thought that if he created enough mayhem, the church would be closed and the bequest would revert to his family."

"Obviously he knew nothing about the staying power of the traditional church," Lucy commented. "But Lester, you and Pete seemed to be there at the same time as Mr. Miller. So Lester, begging your pardon, why didn't you see him coming down from the tower?"

Lester looked at Pete. Pete looked at Lester, fingers tapping lightly on his drum. Lester sighed. "Weeeell, my buddy and I weren't exactly right at the scene at that time. We'd done our washing up with the hose, like I said. But then another buddy yelled up from the side street that some Starbuckers were giving out free coffee coupons at our solicitation corner. So we went down to grab a few, and I left my shirt where it was. We were coming back to get it when the janitor nabbed us."

Joe clapped his hands together. "Very concise and succinct, Lester. And if you and Pete would like to become janitors' assistants, you'd better learn to call him Mr. Henry."

"Become what?" Lester's head swiveled around.

"And let's continue the applause for my darling wife," Joe continued, putting his arm around Mary. "She's talked Henry into taking partial retirement, so there'll be funds to pay his apprentices ... that is, if they can keep themselves from wandering off to cadge free coupons and hang around street corners."

As Lucy and Lisa clapped, the two men went to huddle in the corner. Joe knew there was a good chance they'd turn down the offer or any offer that kept them tethered to a specific place.

Joe spoke louder to be heard over the applause. "And then, AND THEN, when Mary visited Mark Miller before he got out of jail, he broke down crying and apologized. He claims he didn't see either Clare or Father Robert before throwing the stones. I guess the prosecutor will have to sort that out. Anyway, Mary would have made a great detective; people see her coming and start confessing and promising to make amends."

Mary snuggled closer to Joe. "I'm going to recommend to Father Robert that the vestry give the family enough money to pay off their debts," Mary said.

"That's very generous dear, but none of us know how much debt there is and what it's for. I doubt the vestry would vote to help the family rather than repair the tower."

Mary grabbed a cookie. "I guess you're right. I just feel so sorry for Audrey. Neola should have spent more time teaching her daughter how to pick appropriate husbands and less at society dances."

"Maybe we can pass the hat or something," said Lester from the corner. "I personally collected one hundred dollars in donations at the funeral." The others looked at him. "I was just getting ready to turn it in," he added, pulling a wad out of his pocket.

"Oh thank you, Mr. Lester," said Daniel, speaking from

the entryway, standing next to his father. "Maybe we'll also have enough for real bells to put in the tower. My dad learned how to play carillons while he was living in England. He met Mr. Evans in Minnesota at the AIDS hospice; that's how he found out that Grace church has a good organ and nice people. When this job came open he let me know with an anonymous letter. But he lives in Portland, Oregon, now. And he's decided he can be my father again. He's sorry he stayed away so long, but he's always kept track of how I was doing and helped me from behind the scenes. Oh my. I just said a lot."

Tears glistening in his eyes, Peter LaSalle said, "I just want to add, thank you all from the bottom of my heart for serving as Daniel's family."

Daniel had been moving up and down on his toes during this little speech. "I thank you all, too. But back to the tower bells. Once my dad teaches us to ring them, Grace Church can be put on the schedule."

"What schedule is that, dear?" Mary asked.

"Oh. You don't know. The churches have to take turns, because there's a noise ordinance that only allows one church at a time to ring its bells on Sundays. My idea is for our bells, which will be real bells, to peal the week after the Cathedral's electric ones. Then everyone will say that ours sound much better.

"Oh, and I just thought of one more thing …. The pigeons are afraid of the bells, so they'll stay away from the tower. Henry won't have to clean up those white spots anymore."

Father Robert's voice drifted down from the stairway. "Amen to that!"

Photograph by Paul Hannah

After retiring from a career as a "government bureaucrat" serving primarily in the criminal justice system, **Kathie Deviny** studied creative writing. Essays focusing on her treatment for breast cancer and life as the spouse of an Episcopal priest have been published in the *Seattle Times*, *Episcopal Life, Cure* magazine, and *Faith, Hope and Healing* by Bernie Siegel.

Kathie was Features Editor of her high school newspaper and originally planned a career in journalism. After realizing she was too shy to chase after stories, she followed her mother's career path and earned Bachelor's and Master's degrees in social work, attending UC Berkeley and the University of Washington. She nurtured her journalistic ambitions by developing a program at the Monroe, WA, prison which produced a magazine in cooperation with community volunteers.

Death in the Memorial Garden, her first work of fiction, reflects her love of the cozy-style mystery. Her other loves are gardening, choral singing, and locating bargains at her church's thrift shop, where she volunteers. Kathie lives with her now-retired husband, Paul; they divide their time between California and Western Washington.

You can find Kathie online at Deviny.camelpress.com.